Firefly Lies

Morgan Matthews

THE BIOGRAPHER

Though the moderately attractive woman sitting across from me in my untidy living room seems friendly enough, I can't help but notice that all-too-familiar pain in the pit of my stomach as she takes a drink from her personalized water bottle. I try to focus on something other than the fact that she will inevitably begin posing questions. The initials on her bottle read 'SBJ.' I know what both the 'S' and 'J' stand for. I have only spoken to Sadie Jordan twice before we made plans for her to conduct this interview.

She's a bit younger than I was expecting—forty, maybe. She has to have at least ten years on me. Her blonde hair is tied up tightly in a bun atop her head. Not a 'messy' bun, such as the kind I usually sport around the house—and, if I'm being honest, the grocery store and car line for my five-year-old's school. Sadie's bun, on the other hand, has not a single hair out of place.

What could the 'B' stand for? Beth? Barbara? Beatrice?

Sadie Blythe Jordan rests her bottle gingerly on the coffee table. That's what I've decided her middle name is—*Blythe*. Maybe I'm just reaching because I wish I knew more about the woman than I do. We are about to delve deep into *my* life, yet I know very little about her.

My next-door neighbor set this up. Keira has been pestering me for over a year to meet with her biographer friend, Sadie. Up until now, I've managed to put her off.

Keira and her husband are the best kind of neighbors. Their lawn is always manicured to perfection. They keep an eye on the house for us when we're out of town, and she never hesitates to step in and help out with my girls when needed.

I notice a half-eaten pear sitting on the area rug which covers our hardwood flooring–rotting away. I roll my eyes as I nonchalantly kick it out of Sadie's line of sight. My daughters are five and three, and predictably less than helpful when it comes to keeping our home tidy. I wish I'd had more time to pick up the living room after they left. Their father and I agree that they shouldn't be here while Sadie and I talk. We don't want to risk them overhearing.

Though, admittedly, I can't place all the blame on the girls for the mess. Our dining room is being utilized as an art studio of sorts. Even still, one of my smaller wooden easels is currently housed in a corner of the kitchen, with my paints scattered about the breakfast table. An unfinished painting of a local chapel rests longingly atop the easel, and I can't help but to wish I could get back to work.

"Okay, Greer. Are you ready?" Sadie asks with a comforting smile as she pulls one of those yellow legal pads from her shoulder bag and positions herself to take notes.

"I am," I respond, *lying*.

"So, how much do you know about what I do?" she asks.

"Keira only told me that you've written several biographies."

"Yes. She didn't tell me too much about you. I really prefer to go into these interviews blind—no preconceived notions," she adds.

I nod. I haven't told Keira everything, and I really don't know if I'll be able to get there with Sadie either. Keira only has bits and pieces—and I've known *her* for years.

"Well then, where would you like to start?" Sadie asks as I hear the subtle click of her pen.

I take a breath. "Before we get started, I want you to understand that I was just a child at the time—*when this all occurred.* All I can do is relay a sequence of events for you, just as I recall them. The perspective in which I viewed the world was that of a child."

Sadie nods. "Understood," she replies, catching my eyes as she looks up.

CHAPTER ONE

"I just don't get it, Dad," my father says, as he hands Grandpa a second helping of peach cobbler (topped with a scoop of vanilla ice cream so tall it rivals even those over-the-top desserts at fancy restaurants).

"What don't you get, Owen? Your aunt is nearly seventy–she can't be expected to handle that whole estate on her own. That was always Carl's thing," he replies, hovering over his dessert like a vulture ready to attack its prey.

Grandpa Frank has always been very matter-of-fact. I must admit it amuses me how Dad gets so flustered when he and his father don't see eye to eye. Dad is used to being in charge–at home, and at work. I guess you'd say he's a natural-born leader. But so is Grandpa.

I take a seat back at the table once finished with dishes. Dad always wants plates cleared before we can move on to dessert.

Grandpa Frank gives me a wink as Dad hands me my own bowl of cobbler, though I must admit I'm a little disappointed at the helping size.

"So, Greer–how does it feel to be twelve?" Grandpa asks, trying to change the subject.

"Mmm… I guess it feels about like it did to be eleven."

He gives me a knowing glance as Dad finally joins us.

"Whether you like it or not, this is something we need to talk about," my father says, refusing to let it go. "I just don't think it's necessary for you to move in with Aunt Cece. The estate is clear on the other side of town."

"It's just a thirty-minute drive, son. And she asked for my help. With Carl gone now, she needs me."

"But is it necessary for you to *live* there?" my dad protests.

"You know how big that place is. And how much real estate they own. Not to mention with Carl not leaving a will, it makes things that much more complicated," Grandpa responds calmly.

"Cece was his *wife*. I don't see what could be complicated," my father adds decidedly. "Not to mention that Carl always *did* have the best CPAs and attorneys working for him; I'm sure they'll help her out. Though it *is* surprising no one ever convinced him to write out a will."

"Well, I suppose he thought he had time for all that—not even seventy yet. Cece said they weren't aware of his heart condition—not until the end at least."

My father nods before finally taking a bite of his dessert.

"Your aunt will have plenty of help, but she needs someone she can trust right now," Grandpa Frank continues. "And it's not just for her sake. There's the employees, the tenants… lots of people to think about."

Grandpa has always been very protective of his sister, despite her being nearly ten years his senior. It's been a few weeks since her husband, Carl, passed, and

Dad still isn't sold on the idea of Grandpa moving in with her. Personally, I don't think it will be so bad. Aunt Cece could really use the help.

Grandpa Frank has lived with us since my mother passed away just a few months after I was born. Although I do hate to lose him, I wouldn't mind visiting Aunt Cece's house more often (if you could even call it a house).

"She's never been too involved with the business side of things, and I wouldn't want to see her overwhelmed with it all," Grandpa adds emphatically.

My father sighs, as though conceding. "I suppose you're right. Selfishly, I wonder how well I'll be able to balance work and a homelife, without you here holding down the fort."

"You have to know I'll still be around, son. After all, my favorite granddaughter lives here. If it weren't for her, I would have ditched *you* long ago," he says with a grin.

THE BIOGRAPHER

"So, Frank *did* move in with his sister?" Sadie asks, scribbling away on her yellow legal pad.

"He did. It was kind of tough at first, but I got used to it. We visited him at Langley Estates a lot."

"Did you enjoy spending time with your aunt?"

"*I did.* Aunt Cece was just the most gracious person. The kitchen pantry was always fully-stocked. Her home may as well have been Narnia with all there was to explore."

"How did your father adjust?" she asks.

"He always worked a lot. So, I was on my own most of the time, but Grandpa checked in with me constantly," I reply.

Sadie finally takes a moment to look up from her notes–making eye contact before probing further.

"May I ask how your mother passed?" The hesitation in Sadie's voice is apparent.

I suppose it's only natural she would want to know how Grandpa came to live with us in the first place, but asking me to talk about Emma is like asking me to open a box I've had buried in a closet for years. I take comfort in knowing that it's there for me to revisit anytime I want, but the idea of opening it up in front of a stranger sounds painfully odd.

"My father always told me that she was having a tough time emotionally after my birth. One day, she was found… *she died in the bathtub.*"

Sadie nods sympathetically before focusing her attention back to her notepad. I wish I could know what she's thinking. Is she judging my living room with the toys and board books scattered along the floor? I don't know why I let Keira talk me into this.

"So, Frank living with his sister worked out… and you and your father were okay on your own?" she asks.

I nod. "Yes, for a few years, anyway," I reply, as countless memories bombard my brain like an unexpected hailstorm. "I was fifteen when…" I begin, taking a moment to gather my thoughts.

"What happened at fifteen?" Sadie asks, following a pause.

CHAPTER TWO

It's been three years since Cece's husband died. Three years since Grandpa Frank moved in with his sister to help out.

Aunt Cecilia sits across from me. Her looks have always been second to none, seemingly immune to the ravages of time. Her thick, gray hair is always styled to perfection—usually donning a thick braid across her hairline, acting as a headband of sorts. In her younger days she had worn it cascading down her back, but transitioned to more updos in recent years.

As I look at her now, sobbing uncontrollably into her embroidered handkerchief, I want nothing more than to find the words to comfort her. It's not fair—losing her husband like that, and *now* her only brother. It's hard to pay any mind to my own grief as I watch her suffering the way she is.

It has been two days since my Grandpa Frank's funeral. Dad and I have spent a lot of time at the estate since he died—helping with funeral plans and greeting friends who have come by to pay their respects. Dad has been holding up pretty well, considering. He hasn't let me see him cry. He thinks he needs to be strong for me, but I wish he'd let me help more than he does.

"Owen, could you get that please?" Cece asks, as the sound of knocking can be heard from the front of the house.

"Leon and Ben have been letting people through the front gate all day. Surely the visits will slow down soon. I know you need to get some rest," my father says, rising from his armchair.

"I do hope so… but then again, the visits help keep my mind off things," she replies, hurriedly wiping tears from her face.

Leon and Ben are the groundskeepers at Langley. I suppose Leon is about my aunt's age, and exactly what you might expect the stereotypical groundskeeper to look like. His wrinkled skin leaves no doubt as to his time spent outdoors. His 'salt and pepper' locks are always combed back, though with plenty of strands out of place. He doesn't really interact much with anyone. It seems as though my Aunt Cece is the only person he's comfortable around.

Leon has worked at the estate for over twenty years. My aunt has said that he was very close with her late husband. Nothing seems to happen on the grounds without Leon's knowledge or say-so, especially considering he lives in a small cottage near the back of the property.

Ben, on the other hand, has only worked at Langley for about a year. Aunt Cece felt that some of the more strenuous manual labor was getting to be too much for Leon to handle on his own, despite his objections. Grandpa Frank helped her interview several candidates before she finally decided to hire him.

Ben is in his early twenties, and painfully oblivious to how attractive he is. I do my best to ignore how his rich, umber skin radiates in the sun as he works outdoors. I fear that one day either my dad or aunt will catch my wayward gaze as we walk the grounds.

I hear Cece greeting her guests as I make my way through the kitchen and out the side door. The cool air washes over me like a wave as I step foot onto the steps which lead to the yard. I don't wish to face the pleasantries and hugging that would surely commence should I step back inside in search of a jacket.

Strands of Christmas lights emit a subtle glow as the sun sets slowly in the distance. It must have taken Ben ages to put all of these lights up. It wouldn't surprise me though if Grandpa had stepped in to help. Christmas was always his favorite.

"How's it going?" I hear as I descend the concrete steps. I jump involuntarily–startled by the sudden disruption in the calm of the evening.

"Oh. Sorry! I didn't mean to scare you. *I'm Thomas*," he says reassuringly. "Anne-Marie's son."

Anne-Marie is the head housekeeper at Langley. I've met her a few times but we've never had much of a chance to talk. Though there are other housekeepers who filter in and out, Anne-Marie always seems as though in a hurry to complete her work for the day.

"Can I assume you're Greer? Mrs. Cecilia talks about you a lot. And of course, your grandpa did too," he says, his eyes shifting momentarily to the ground as though in sympathy.

"Yes, that's me," I respond, feeling a bit silly at my initial reaction to his presence. I've always struggled when it comes to being aware of my surroundings. I tend to get lost in my thoughts at regular intervals throughout the day. "Did you need me to get Cece for you?" I ask.

"No, that's okay. My mom did your aunt's grocery shopping for her earlier, but this bag was left in the car," he says, handing me a plastic bag filled with what look to be pantry items. "Mom asked me to drop it off."

I'm surprised he's old enough to drive. He doesn't seem any older than me, though I guess he *must* be at least sixteen. His light hair is thick and wavy, cascading across his forehead in a heap. He stares up at me with his gray-blue eyes as though we've been friends for ages.

"Well, thanks for stopping by. I'm sure Cece will appreciate it."

"Yeah, no problem. I'm surprised we haven't met before. I'm here a lot after school," he replies, continuing the conversation.

Dad and I have always visited on the weekends. I didn't even realize Anne-Marie had any children—*of course, she doesn't say much.*

"Frank was a great guy. I was really sorry to hear what happened."

"Thank you. It was pretty unexpected with him being so healthy," I respond, realizing I haven't actually had a chance to talk about him since the day of his stroke.

Thomas nods before nervously kicking at the dirt beneath his feet. "So, where did you get your red hair from? I know it wasn't your grandpa," he asks bluntly.

I'm not really used to interacting with guys my own age—are they all this prone to blurting? I've been homeschooled since I hit second grade. The public school system tried to accommodate me as best they could, but it just didn't work out. I was bored to tears every day until

Dad decided to hire me a tutor. I finished up my senior year of high school a few months ago, and I've now moved on to taking college courses online.

"Uh… well, my mother had red hair," I reply awkwardly. I'm not sure if I should be offended by his question or not. As a kid I genuinely despised my hair, and did everything I could to conceal it under hats and scarves–anything to distract from the color. I didn't want to stand out. I just wanted to disappear. The fact that I had an in-home tutor wasn't exactly the norm for children my age–or *any* children for that matter.

I've had the same group of friends for years. Dad and I are members of the Rutledge Country Club. My summers are spent mostly running up our tab at the clubhouse grill, ordering ICEEs and sour straws as Dad golfs with friends and business contacts. The club swimming pool is where my friends and I spend most of our time. We also enjoy taking a golf cart for a drive around the property in the afternoons.

I'm the only one in our social group to not attend either public or private school, so there's very little opportunity for me to meet new people. Though I must admit, with all the drama that seemingly permeates the high school experience, I count myself lucky to have avoided it.

My friends from the country club have been good to me, and so have their parents. My father travels a lot for work. I like to refer to him as a traveling salesman– like the kind that used to go door-to-door selling anything and everything. I once read a book which referred to men in that line of work as *peddlers*. Grandpa Frank and I got a good kick out of calling Dad a peddler for the better part of a month.

He's actually in the frozen food market–selling products to grocery stores all over the country. We've always had Grandpa to take care of things at home (at least, up until three years ago) while Dad's away, but I've also spent my fair share of time at friends' houses. Sleepovers which last the better part of a week are not outside the norm for me. I will confess that it can be a nice change of pace. *My house is quiet.* There's zero drama. No siblings to squabble with over a stolen blouse or filched leftovers from the refrigerator.

Grandpa Frank has always filled in the gaps where Dad fell short. He was never lacking in conversation– regularly materializing life lessons out of any situation. Our talks were what I missed the most when he moved in with Cece.

"Well, I like it. You don't see that deep of a red too often," Thomas responds. I know we just met, but I can tell he's being sincere.

"Thanks… I've come to appreciate it over the years–especially since I convinced Grandpa to quit calling me 'Gingersnap,'" I quip.

At this, we share a laugh. I have a feeling that he can easily imagine Grandpa saying such a thing. I realize it's the first time I've laughed in days, though I can't help but feel guilty–like maybe it's wrong to find anything funny right now.

I kind of hate that Thomas is just so dang statuesque. I shouldn't be out here having a perfectly enjoyable conversation with some guy a mere year or so older than myself. I should be inside comforting the bereaved–especially Cece. She doesn't seem like herself, even more so than I'd expect.

"Well, thanks again. I'll let my aunt know you stopped by," I say, turning back towards the door.

"No problem. It was nice meeting you, Greer."

As I put up groceries, I can hear the sound of Cece sobbing in the other room. I wish I had different clothes here to change into. It seems like we've been taking visitors all day, and I suddenly feel the full weight of my exhaustion.

Dad always has me dress like we're going to court. Dresses falling just below the knee, panty hose, and a slight heel is my go-to outfit. I used to think he was overcompensating because I've never had a mom around, but I've come to realize it's more than just that. He, himself, has always worn a suit and tie to work, insisting presentation is everything. He's a big believer in the importance of making a good first impression.

Dad has always relished in opportunities to acquire new skills, such as styling my hair when I was young. He could have easily cut it short and let it be, but he taught himself to fix it, in order to spare me from any unnecessary embarrassment.

I slip off my shoes as I quietly close the pantry door, so as not to disturb Cece and her guests. I hear Dad offering to grab her more tissues as I take a seat at one of the barstools which line the granite countertop. I want nothing more than to be at home in bed–binge-watching literally anything to get my mind off all of this–especially Grandpa Frank.

There's a sudden thump just behind me, followed by an audible gasp. It isn't loud; I may just be hearing things. I turn toward the door. I'd left it open to the outdoors, though the screen is closed. I see the groundskeeper, Leon, at the steps which lead to the grass below. He's holding tightly to the railing as though he'd slipped and just managed to catch himself. He and I make eye contact, however briefly. I try to speak, but find myself inexplicably tongue-tied. Leon then turns quickly– disappearing from my line of sight.

CHAPTER THREE

It seems like my life has been defined by death. All fifteen years of life, plagued with the tragedy of my mother's death mere months following my birth. I was spared the details when I was younger. Grandpa Frank told me my mother was simply too 'perfect' to stay here on this earth for long–*too* beautiful, *too* kind, *too* sensitive, and far too loving. *How was I ever naïve enough to buy into that crap?*

I've studied every photo of Emma I could get my hands on over the years. She really *was* beautiful–long red hair that bleached in the sun, turning the top a delicate shade of strawberry-blonde. Her dark green eyes and fair skin were nothing less than enchanting against the backdrop of her wedding day. I'm really not sure *what* she saw in my dad, at least not looks-wise. There's no question he married out of his league, but I suppose he can be charming. His looks have thankfully grown much more distinguished with age. Isn't it just like a man to age like Benjamin Button?

She wore a vintage ivory gown with long sleeves– appropriate for December nuptials. Delicate buttons lined the entirety of the back, which draped gracefully along the floor. The dress currently resides in my father's closet– ominously preserved in one of those boxes the cleaners place it in following the big day. He says she would want me to have it, but it's hard to imagine myself ever wanting to commit to *anything* for a lifetime, especially a fallible man. I'm confident the dress will remain in that box, forever a reminder of a time when my mother was indeed happy. That is, until she wasn't.

As I said, my life has been defined by death. Perhaps it shouldn't be such a shock to watch as Aunt Cece's mangled body is—at long last—freed from her car which rests at the bottom of an embankment mere miles from her home. Dad and I were just finishing up dinner when he got the call. The restaurant tonight is a family tradition—*Leila's*—same as every Christmas Eve. Though it is the first year it's just the two of us.

It must have been at least half an hour ago that we left the restaurant. We made it here as fast as we could, but the ice and snow didn't leave much room for error. Dad tried to remain calm, but I could see the agony written all over his face as he tossed some cash onto our table. Sans a bill, he must have left at least double the cost of our meal.

As I stand peering into the darkness, the paramedics place my aunt on a stretcher and begin hoisting her up the steep hill below my feet. By the time we made it to the scene, a small crowd had formed near the point at which her car broke clear through the railing. They weren't trying to help, just recording the scene via their cell phones—completely detached. Almost as if they were watching it play out on their television screens rather than right in front of them.

Her Honda Civic is indistinguishable—covered in both the black of the night, as well as the white of new-fallen snow. It resembles a crumpled piece of aluminum foil more so than it does a vehicle. No one could have survived this. Especially not someone my aunt's age. I suppose it's more of a formality at this point that she be transported via an ambulance rather than a hearse.

Dad is speaking with a police officer–hanging his head in despair. He is clearly doing his best to keep his composure. It has been just two weeks since Grandpa Frank's funeral. We are nowhere near past the shock of losing him so unexpectedly–and now this. Now Cece is gone too–Grandpa's only sibling.

I catch one final glimpse of her before the doors of the ambulance are shut tight. Blood covers her face. Her gray hair is caked and matted. I can tell it's her, but yet at the same time–she no longer looks like Cece. I *know* she's gone.

One thing I've always admired about my aunt is her humility. She and her husband, Carl, made some particularly lucrative real estate investments several decades ago, and as a result enjoyed the security of a bank account rivaling that of a small country. They were rich, yet materialism just wasn't in them. Langley Estates has employed a lot of people for many years, and my aunt and uncle have treated them well.

They were very well-known and respected in their town–particularly since they own about half of it. Despite the burning sensation in my eyes, I watch as the ambulance leaves with Cece. I doubt the paramedics know who she is. She doesn't look like herself. And who would guess that a multi-millionaire would pass away in the middle of a snowstorm, driving a Honda Civic? No pomp and circumstance. No Rolls-Royce. No driver. Just Aunt Cece losing control of her car as a result of the ice and snow on Christmas Eve.

THE BIOGRAPHER

"That must have been very difficult–losing your grandfather, and then your aunt just weeks later. Both unexpectedly." Sadie pauses. I'm not sure if she's asking a question or merely making a statement.

"It was," I respond. I'm not really comfortable yet sitting in silence with her, so I have to fill the void.

"What did the police determine?" she asks.

"It was after dark. She really shouldn't have been driving after dark, especially not in a snowstorm. The roads were slick and the car hydroplaned. She couldn't regain control and busted through the railing. She wasn't far from home, but it was all downhill–she likely picked up a lot of speed before the car went down the embankment."

"How was she handling Frank's death… before the accident?" she probes.

I know what Sadie is getting at.

"Not too well, honestly. I had never seen her like that. She was devastated when Carl died, but Grandpa helped pull her through. Then when *he* was gone, it just… it changed her. We offered her help, but nothing seemed to make a difference. Though I *have* always felt that had she not passed, she would have found a new normal… eventually. She would have found a reason to start living again. After all, it had only been two weeks."

I pause, anticipating her next question–though I already know what it will be.

"Did you think there was any chance it was *intentional?* That she could have taken her own life?" Sadie asks hesitantly, clearly trying to remain respectful.

"No," I reply flatly.

She seems a bit surprised at the matter-of-factness in my response. "When was the last time you saw her, before the night of the accident?"

It isn't lost on me that she refers to the wreck as an *accident* following my response to her previous question. She isn't pushing the subject–probably because of what she knows about my mother. She thinks it will offend me–trigger me somehow.

"Dad and I decided to stop by Langley before finishing up our Christmas shopping. It was the evening before her wreck. I knew we wouldn't have time to make it by the next day (on Christmas Eve). We had a lot of traditions to uphold, Dad and I–most of them pretty ridiculous," I respond.

"What were your traditions?" Sadie asks. She seems genuinely interested, which I find a bit surprising.

"We'd always catch a matinee at the movie theater–sometimes it was Christmas-y, but most of the time it wasn't. We would drive around and choose a random home we thought had the best light display."

Sadie is writing feverishly as I speak.

"We'd place a homemade congratulatory sign in their front yard. If only we could have witnessed their reactions. I imagine they had a lot of questions, like: What is the Tipton Family Christmas Light Contest? Is that a real thing?"

Sadie looks up from her notepad, placing her hand over her mouth to stifle her laughter.

"We'd finish the day off with dinner at Leila's—which is where we got the call. It was always Grandpa's favorite tradition. In fact, all of it started with him. Dad and I were just along for the ride—well, especially Dad. That year, after Grandpa passed away so close to Christmas, it was important to me to keep the traditions going."

"So, it was the evening *before* Christmas Eve that you last saw Cece alive?" Sadie asks, glancing up from her lap.

"Yes. She was in no way ready to leave her house yet, and I wanted to get our gift to her before Christmas."

"How did she seem that night?"

"She was upset," I reply. "But I wouldn't say any more so than she'd been since the funeral—at least not at first. The housekeeper cooked her meals most weeknights. When we arrived, Anne-Marie wasn't quite finished up, so Cece and Dad spoke in the den while I joined Thomas in the kitchen."

I can tell Sadie wants me to continue without her prompting, but there just wasn't anything I noticed that night to suggest something was amiss. Though I may *have* to keep going if she doesn't ask another question soon. I hate the uncomfortable silence that permeates every crevice of the living room as she records my words. *My story.* A tale which I've spent half of my life trying to forget.

"Did you spend much time there that evening?" she continues.

"No. Cece was pretty emotional, so it didn't seem like an appropriate time to give her a present. We just left it there for her."

"Did your father notice anything was off?" she asks.

"On our way home, he did mention that he was worried about her. Said she looked like she had lost some weight. Anne-Marie had confirmed that Cece wasn't eating well, regardless of what she cooked."

"But, neither of you suspected she might do anything to harm herself?" Sadie asks.

I thought we had already covered this.

"No," I respond, a bit defiantly.

CHAPTER FOUR

Though the bitter cold makes its way through every crevice of my winter attire–I haven't moved a muscle in at least half an hour or so. I was relieved Dad agreed to transport my trampoline over to Langley when we moved in; I wasn't sure if he would. I've always found it strangely calming–lying flat, arms stretched out as though floating on water. I wouldn't dare to actually jump until the weather warms up a bit.

I watch as Ben and Leon take down Christmas lights. Ben stands atop a ladder–passing off strings of lights to Leon as they work. It's already three weeks past New Years. I suppose they couldn't put off the task any longer, no matter how much we're all still hurting.

Leon has been as unpleasant as ever since the wreck, though I try not to judge him too harshly. *I know he and my aunt were close.* Ben, on the other hand, has been a huge help to Dad and I these past few weeks. His brute strength and upbeat disposition have both proven invaluable during this unexpected transition we're all trying to navigate.

After her husband passed, Cece named Grandpa Frank as her beneficiary. He spent the last three years of his life at Langley–handling all of my aunt's affairs. He learned the business. Built rapport with tenants and business partners–never wanting them to worry that anything might fall through the cracks with Carl gone. It was always meant to be *him* to take over things at Langley, eventually.

Cece was a good bit older than Grandpa, and in much more fragile health. I don't think any of us could have imagined that he would be the one to pass first. Though, we also couldn't have imagined they would *both* be gone mere weeks apart.

I've done everything I can to help, but the lion's share of the burden has been unceremoniously placed on my father's shoulders. He never expected to take over Langley. I don't believe it was something he even considered until Grandpa's death—especially considering that Grandpa Frank was as healthy as they come (until of course he wasn't).

It has all been a bit of a blur. Grandpa's stroke. Cece's wreck. The funerals. Moving out of the only home I've ever known and into an estate which could easily accommodate a couple dozen occupants. Dad having to quit his job in sales in order to take over at Langley.

Dad could have helped Cece hire someone to handle her affairs. She wasn't in it alone. There just wasn't any time for things to settle down after Grandpa's death. It was still so raw—none of us wanted to burden her with anything else.

"WHAT do you think you're doing!?" I hear. I'm still looking up at the sky (thinking about nothing at all; yet also *everything*, all at once). I lift my head slowly in anticipation.

It's Leon. He's been yelling at Ben a lot since Cece passed away. He may be his superior, but I really hate to see Ben being used as his own personal punching bag.

"You trying to get yourself killed!?" Leon continues.

"No sir, Mr. Leon. The pitch isn't too high right there where I jumped from. Don't worry–I landed right on my feet," Ben responds politely.

"Yeah, I *saw* you land. Don't you pull those stunts around here!" Leon barks.

"Sorry about that. Won't happen again," Ben replies, clearly being sincere. It seems as though he lets everything Leon says roll right off his back, though I don't know *how*.

I sit up just in time to watch Anne-Marie's car make its way down the long, winding driveway towards the estate. Dad and I have relied on both Leon and Anne-Marie a lot lately. With Leon knowing all the workings of the grounds both backward and forward, and Anne-Marie running the house–I don't know how we could manage without them.

Admittedly, I've been judgmental of Langley's head housekeeper at times. She tends to be strict–especially when it comes to Thomas. He's sixteen and yet she requires him to join her at the house every day after school. I suppose it's just hard for me to relate; Dad has always given me plenty of space. But Thomas doesn't seem to mind. And she *is* at least polite (unlike Leon).

It must be nearly nine o'clock if Anne-Marie's here. I lower myself off the trampoline just as Ben and Leon are about to move on to the other side of the house. Though only a few feet off the ground, I wouldn't dare jump–not after how Leon just scolded Ben. I prefer to remain off of Leon's radar.

A new semester just kicked off at school, so there's not a lot of work for me to do quite yet. Professors tend to take it slow the first week, allowing time for students to add and drop classes.

Thomas and I have been spending a lot of time together. His school started back a week earlier than my courses, and we've already fallen into a routine upon his arrival each day. I find myself regularly checking the time, wondering why it's taking so long for three o'clock to get here so we can pick up where we left off the day before.

It frustrates me how his sarcastic comments and witty comebacks *don't* turn me off of him. I detest the way his blonde mop of hair always falls perfectly across his forehead, and how his eyes seem to pierce right through me every time he glances in my direction. It's all a bit corny and embarrassing.

"Good morning, Greer," Anne-Marie says cheerfully as I enter the kitchen. "The boys are taking down the lights I see. Guess that means I should probably get started on the Christmas tree today," she says with a sigh. At least *she* seems to be in an especially good mood.

I think we've all been reluctant to change anything at Langley from the way Cece left it. We haven't even touched her bedroom. There were more than enough rooms for both Dad and I to choose from when we moved over our things. We've slowly been selling and giving away most of our own furniture. We just don't have any use for it anymore; Langley is furnished much nicer than ours ever was.

That's not to say our home wasn't nice. A four-bedroom overlooking the lake isn't exactly something to turn your nose up at. It's just that, no matter where we lived before, *any* home would have a hard time comparing to Langley, or its furnishings. My aunt was an excellent decorator. She never purchased anything until she found a piece she 'couldn't live without'—even if that meant leaving a wall or corner bare for a while.

Langley Estates is a big part of the history of the town in which it is located. So, although Cece couldn't have been less ostentatious if she tried, it's practically a necessity that the home maintain certain standards in order to remain in its current state. Much of the grand, antique furniture has been with the house long before Carl and Cece took over the residency. My aunt felt strongly that it was her duty to preserve such history, to the absolute best of her ability.

I used to love visiting the estate—spending time with Carl and Cece. Their presence always made the home warm and inviting, despite its inherent eeriness. Though, I expect that particular feeling comes with *most* houses this old—imagined or not. The wood floors creek. Drafts cause doors to open and shut on their own. I don't believe in ghosts—never have. But even *I* have to admit I find it a bit unnerving to wander the upstairs halls and bedrooms on my own. It helps when Thomas is here; he knows the layout much better than I do.

It's hard not to wish Dad and I could have stayed in our own home following Cece's death. We discussed it, but it just wasn't practical. We lived thirty minutes away, and he needed to be here. My whole life changed over the course of a few short weeks. I don't want to be selfish, but I'm grieving the loss of my previous life, in addition to the loss of my grandfather and aunt.

I feel more for my father than I do for myself. He has always loved his job in sales. He's a social person, and loves traveling for work. He wasn't prepared for this. *How could he have been?* He spends most of his days on the phone in Carl's old office. From the few conversations I've overheard, it seems as though he's mostly trying to gain the confidence and trust of tenants and business partners–dozens of them. Sometimes it feels like he's trying to reassure himself just as much as them that he has everything under control.

He's also been meeting with Cece's attorney, Mr. Ackerman. It will probably take them months to get everything settled, if not longer. We also see Rory pretty often–my aunt's CPA. The guy would probably be handsome if he'd just lose the mustard-colored button-up shirt and non-coordinating, magenta tie combination he seems so passionately committed to. What's worse though is the pocket protector which houses various pens, pencils, and highlighters–all readily accessible at a moment's notice.

"Would you like some help taking down the tree later?" I ask as Anne-Marie unloads the dishwasher. The artificial Christmas tree adorned with fancy gold and blue ornaments stands in the 'formal' living room–ten feet high at least. The height is certainly fitting for the space. The ceilings at Langley seem to stretch overnight–higher each time I look up.

"Well, of course you're welcome to," she responds. "But it's really no trouble. I've put up and taken down that tree for so many years now I think I could do it in my sleep. I've got a fairly decent system in place, I do believe."

She may have turned me down, but I think this is the longest conversation Anne-Marie and I have ever had. For some reason, I feel the need to try and win her over.

There's also a small Christmas tree placed atop a side table in the room just off the kitchen. I recently heard it referred to as the 'keeping' room—an *informal* living room meant to be a place to 'keep' children in one's line of sight while in the kitchen, according to Thomas at least. Unlike the fancy department-store-worthy tree decked out in coordinating ornaments, the one in the keeping room stands a mere three feet at best (hence its placement off the ground). None of the ornaments match. Most are older. There are even a few handmade pieces I gifted to Cece and Carl as a kid. It really is sweet they kept them—as my art left something to be desired back then.

My aunt and uncle never did have any children of their own, though I'm uncertain if it was by choice or not. And with me being an only child, I suppose I was as close as they had.

"Good morning, Owen," Anne-Marie says, greeting my father with a smile as he makes his way into the kitchen. He's wearing a white shirt, the top few buttons loose. He looks as though he hasn't slept in days. His hair is a mess, and I notice a touch of embarrassment in his expression at Anne-Marie's sentiment.

"Oh, Anne-Marie. Good morning. Sorry. I didn't realize you were here. I must have fallen asleep at my desk sometime early this morning," he says, trying in vain to smooth out the wrinkles in his shirt.

He pours himself a cup of coffee–though I doubt anything but sleep will remedy his current state. I can tell that Anne-Marie is trying to be polite as she fails to comment on his disheveled appearance.

"I thought I heard Ben's voice outside the office window earlier," Dad says, a look of confusion plastered across his tired face. "I don't know if I was dreaming or what."

I can't help but to chuckle. "Ben and Leon are out there taking down the Christmas lights."

He nods before taking a sip of coffee from one of Aunt Cece's 1950s-style mugs.

"Can I make you something for breakfast? Eggs? Cinnamon rolls?" Anne-Marie asks, seemingly addressing both of us.

Though I appreciate the offer, it still feels somehow unnatural to have Anne-Marie wait on us. I can tell my father feels the same, as he politely declines. We've fended for ourselves for a long time. And I still think of her as being Aunt Cece's employee–certainly not ours.

Anne-Marie is younger than Dad, though not by much–late thirties maybe. Her hair is always pulled out of her face as she works, though her spiral curls try desperately to break free. She and Thomas don't really favor one another–apart from their distinctive gray-blue eyes.

Thomas confided in me last week that his father passed away when he was young. It's something we have in common I suppose—*being raised by single parents.* When I told him how my mother died a few months after I was born, he promptly labeled us as being a part of the *"dead parent's club."* I *wanted* to be offended, yet wasn't.

***

Thomas arrives at Langley just as Anne-Marie is packing up what's left of the boujee Christmas tree. Somehow the emptiness of the home is now even more apparent. The formal living room is eerily barren, and it's as though what little life and joy were left lingering from the presence of my aunt has now been snuffed out for good.

Thomas carries each of the plastic storage bins through the house and to the detached garage for his mother. The living space features a large brick fireplace with oversized chairs nearby. I've found it to be the perfect spot for reading, especially when there is a fire going.

My new bedroom is undeniably superior to the room I grew up in—though I can't say I'm a fan of the seclusion. Langley has three bedrooms on the first floor, and five on the second. My room is the first at the top of the grand staircase. The large window seat and view of the grounds made it an easy choice. Dad chose a room on the ground floor, close to the office.

Like my father, my personality prohibits me from being on my own for too long. Of course, I have my moments when I'm glad I have access to such privacy. But for the most part, I need to be around people. I feed off the energy—which is why I've enjoyed having Thomas around. No other reason.

As he reaches for the last remaining bin in the living room, I try not to stare as he quickly pushes the hair out of his eyes. I don't like him as more than a friend. I just need *someone* to help occupy my free time. *Someone* to distract me from the pain I feel when I think of Grandpa Frank and Cece. My father doesn't have a spare minute to give right now. I'm not sure Anne-Marie even *likes* me. And I wouldn't dare try to befriend Leon.

Ben always lets me help with the animals when Leon isn't around. Langley is home to dozens of chickens, pigs, goats, rabbits—and one old cow named Gertie who is clearly on her proverbial last leg. Surprisingly, Leon seems to have a soft spot for her. I know she was always my Aunt Cece's favorite too. It's nice having fresh eggs in the refrigerator at all times. Anne-Marie has said that Gertie used to provide milk for the house in her younger days.

Dad and I never had pets, so it's a nice change. He always said our backyard wasn't big enough for a dog. Now that we're surrounded by several acres of land, I'm kind of hoping he'll reconsider—once things settle down.

"It's looking pretty empty in here… were you guys robbed?" Thomas asks as he plops down on the sofa across from me.

"It sure looks that way—*robbed* of the Christmas spirit," I reply.

"Well, it *is* nearly February," he responds, clearly trying to keep himself from cracking a smile.

"That's true. Now all we have to look forward to is the summer," I reply sarcastically.

"Not a fan of the summer?" he asks, raising an eyebrow.

"I mean, I don't *hate* it. Though I do wish the break between school years would happen in the fall or something… so we could all take our vacations in nicer weather."

"Fall would be too cold for the beach; don't you like going to the beach?" he asks, seemingly amused.

"Honestly, *no*. Grandpa took me once when I was young. I sunburned so bad I ended up in the emergency room."

I can tell he thinks I'm kidding.

"*Really*," I reiterate, laughing.

"Dang! And I thought it was bad when I once left my Mickey ears in our hotel room," he responds.

Sometimes I wonder if he is even making an effort to be funny. I once heard an expression—something about God giving with both hands. I never quite understood it until I met Thomas Chambers.

"Did you finish up what you were reading yesterday?" he asks.

"Yep. At two in the morning. I don't like not knowing how it ends."

He grins at me, and I find it suddenly difficult to get back to my current book.

"I guess that's why you're already in college… while I'm still eating lunch in a school cafeteria and have to ask permission to go to the bathroom," he says, rolling his eyes.

"At least *you're* old enough to drive," I push back.

"That's true," he responds before pulling his cell phone from his pocket. "But my mother isn't exactly easy-going about it. If she *were* you wouldn't have to deal with me being over *here* every day."

The words left his mouth, flew straight across the room, and hit me right in the gut. I know he didn't mean to hurt my feelings. He was just trying to express how he wishes Anne-Marie would loosen the reins a little–as she should. But I hoped he might be starting to enjoy his afternoons spent at the estate–since Dad and I moved in.

I try to get back to reading as he scrolls through his phone. I'm sure he has plenty of friends he'd rather be hanging out with after school–maybe even a girlfriend he hasn't mentioned.

The silence is broken as I hear footsteps coming from the hallway.

"Owen, I wish you would let me fix you something to eat," Anne-Marie says as she makes it back to the living room. I turn my head to see my father coming toward us from the opposite direction. He still hasn't fixed himself up. His hair is long enough that he can't get away with not running a brush through it.

It's really not like him at all, but he's been through a lot–and I don't want to push him by bringing it up just yet. I may be grieving too, but at least I don't have the added pressure of carrying the estate all on my own.

"Well, when you have the time. I suppose I do need to eat something before I head to town for a meeting with some of the business partners," he says, resting a hand on my shoulder.

"Coming right up!" Anne-Marie exclaims, heading to the kitchen. She seems so much more chipper when Dad is around.

"Would you want to come to town with me? I could drop you off somewhere while I have my meeting," Dad asks warmly, his tired eyes peering down at me.

Ordinarily I wouldn't want to miss out on the opportunity to spend time with Thomas. I glance over at him before responding. He's still looking at his phone, but I recognize what I believe to be the vaguest hint of disappointment in his expression. I learned the first time I met him he doesn't think much before speaking. In a way, I really don't mind that about him. Some people are so calculated–their every move seemingly choreographed in advance. But not Thomas. I guess that's the downside to meeting someone so genuine–they may hurt your feelings from time to time, intentionally or not.

"Only if *you* agree to take a shower first," I say teasingly. My father laughs–the first I've heard from him in weeks.

"I was thinking the same thing," he replies.

***

I hadn't realized how much I needed time away from the house–away from the constant reminders of Grandpa Frank and Aunt Cece. Dad dropped me off at a nail salon before heading to his meeting. Red and pink streamers hang from the ceiling of the salon. Large cardboard hearts adorn the walls. And a large sign rests on an easel in a corner of the room– *"Valentine's Day Special–Manicure and Pedicure for $59.99 (Offer valid through February 14th)."*

I'm led to the nearest pedicure chair by a woman with dark hair and bright red lips. Her long, acrylic fingernails are painted with a bold shade of lavender polish. As I remove my shoes and take a seat, I notice as two women round a corner, having come from the other side of the salon. They both hold their hands out flat, so as not to ruin their fresh manicures.

As they take a seat in the chairs next to me, I ease my feet slowly into the warm, soapy water. The technician with lavender nails situates herself in front of me as I flip through a booklet of sample polish colors.

"Did Sarah-Beth go out for danceline this year?" the woman sitting directly beside me asks her friend as they carefully open their complimentary bottles of water. They both appear to be in their late-forties or so. Both nicely dressed. One with blonde, shoulder-length hair, and the other with brown locks cascading clear down the middle of her back.

"She did. I'm glad she's found something she enjoys… but if these kids of mine don't start narrowing down their activities soon they're going to cause me to have a breakdown," the brunette answers with a laugh.

I try to focus on something other than their conversation. I don't even mean to eavesdrop, but the salon is otherwise noiseless. It reminds me of riding an elevator alone with strangers–strangers who actually *know* one another. They often decide to fill the uncomfortable silence with conversation whilst an outsider stands a mere foot or so away, silently listening in–whether they want to or not.

I flip through a nearby magazine, hoping to get some ideas for my nails; all I know is that I *do not* want acrylic.

"Oh, did I tell you Ray is meeting with the new owner of Langley today?" the blonde woman asks, causing every inch of my body to transition into a state of heightened alert.

"No! That will be interesting. I wonder what he's like?" her friend asks.

"Well, Ray spoke to Leon a day or two ago… you know–the groundskeeper. He's been there forever. He told Ray that he's not holding out much hope for Mrs. Cecilia's nephew, *Owen*. He seems to think he's just not up to the task; it's a lot to take on. So, obviously Ray and some of the other partners are getting nervous. It almost makes us wonder if we shouldn't just cut ties, now that

Mr. Frank is gone. He was supposed to be the one to take over."

"Goodness," the woman with long, dark hair responds before taking a swig from her water bottle. "I sure do feel bad for the family. They've been through more tragedy in the last few years than most of us get dealt in a lifetime."

"Oh, I agree. But Ray and the others have to think this over as a business decision, nothing personal. We just don't *know* this man. But we *do* know Leon–and if he says that this Owen guy is incompetent, it has to be something to consider." Her friend nods in agreement before they are distracted by a home renovation show on the flat screen TV mounted on the wall across from us.

I remain silent, though my mind has been sent reeling. I look down at my feet as the woman with lavender nails begins rubbing some kind of sea salt on my heels. I feel like I've been hit by a truck, yet no one notices. I'm bleeding out, right here in this nail salon.

I knew that Leon didn't care for us–but I never really took it personally because it seems as though he doesn't like *anyone*. Now, I *know* it's personal. He lacks any first-hand knowledge of the business side of things, yet he's labeling Dad as incompetent. Leon knows that we were thrown into this chaos without warning, after having just lost not one, but *two*, close family members. How could he be so lacking in tact and compassion?

I spend the remainder of my time at the salon agonizing over what I've just overheard. Why would Leon do that to us? To Dad? It makes me wonder the real purpose of this meeting today. Are they trying to feel him out? See if what Leon has been saying is true?

I notice that Dad is already parked outside waiting on me as I sign my receipt. I want to tell him *everything* as I slide into the passenger seat of his car. I show off both my manicure and pedicure as he places my shoes in the backseat.

"Goodness! I bet you're freezing after wearing those Styrofoam flip-flops out," he says as he turns up the heater.

"It's just a few feet out the front door," I answer with a grin. "I'm surprised I didn't have to wait for you. *How was your meeting?*" I inquire, praying I've adequately masked the skepticism in my voice.

"Oh, just fine. It seems like the partners just wanted to get to know me a little better. They had a lot of questions, as they should. We got into a few specifics. And I answered them as best I could, based on what I've learned these past few weeks. But I just asked for their patience as we get through this transition."

I stare down at my cobalt-blue fingernails as we make our way back to Langley. I want to tell him that he should fire Leon immediately. Tell him he's betraying us. Let him know that we can't trust him.

I *want* to tell him, but I just can't burden him with this. He is dealing with enough as it is. And we rely on Leon's expertise. This news may be the proverbial straw that breaks the camel's back. Dad hardly eats, let alone sleeps, since my aunt passed. *I can keep an eye on Leon myself.*

CHAPTER FIVE

Upon our return to the house my father promptly retreats back to his office. Thomas seems as though he's happy to see me. I can tell he feels guilty about what he said before I left, but neither of us mention the exchange. People rarely acknowledge such interactions—and those that do tend to make others uncomfortable.

Any sixteen-year-old guy would feel some sort of resentment for having to join his mother at her work every day after school. I know he likes spending time with me—*otherwise he wouldn't.* Thomas could just as easily bury his nose in his cell phone all afternoon.

He sent me a friend request on Facebook just a few hours after our first meeting at Langley. Then an Instagram follow came soon thereafter. From what I can tell, he's the same guy at his high school that he is when he's with me—confident, smart, pleasant… maybe a tad arrogant.

It's hard not to be a little envious of his life. My friends live over half an hour away now, and I don't have the heart to ask Dad to drive me to see anyone. My friends have all been in touch since the funerals, but I can't pretend things will be the same as they were. I wonder if we'll even keep up our membership at the country club.

"So, why blue?" Thomas asks, as though genuinely interested in the shade of my fingernails. He climbs to the top of a large stack of hay bales which are housed in a covered shed behind the chicken coop.

"*I don't know.* Just a random choice, really."

"Oh, come on. I have no doubt there's some deep-rooted psychological meaning behind your choice of nail color," he quips.

I laugh as he awkwardly slips on the hay beneath his feet. "Do you even know what you're talking about?" I ask. "Like what, some kind of subliminal message that I'm trying to send out into the world?"

"*Of course* I know what I'm talking about. I took Psychology last year," he says with a smirk.

I want to tell him that I took Psychology 101 last semester online–a requirement for all *college* freshmen at my school–but at the risk of sounding conceited, I resist. No one likes a know-it-all, or so I've been told.

"If the color *does* hold a deeper meaning, I promise you that I am blissfully unaware," I respond.

"*Sure* you are," he says, smiling as he jumps from the top of the stack of hay.

"So, is all this for Gertie?" I ask, changing the subject.

"*Sure is.* Leon mostly has Ben take care of the animals these days. Makes me wonder if he even told the guy how much hay to order," he replies. It seems that Thomas has about as much fondness for Leon as I do.

"So, he hasn't been very helpful to Ben since he started working here?" I ask, trying to seem as though less interested than I actually am.

"I don't know… I'm not really around them too much. It just seems like Leon does more griping than teaching."

I wish I could share with Thomas what I overheard today in order to get his thoughts on the matter. But what if he tells his mother? Would Anne-Marie tell Leon that I'm on to him? I don't have any particular reason to believe she *would*, as she seems to really like my dad. But I can't risk it. At least not until I know I can trust Thomas to keep it to himself. Anne-Marie and Leon have worked together for a long time. *Who knows?* Maybe she's been spreading falsehoods too.

I notice that both Ben and Leon are crossing the yard—traveling from the tool shed toward the chicken coop. My eyes must have given it away, as Thomas promptly quits talking and turns to greet them.

"How's it going, *kids?*" Ben asks teasingly.

Leon unceremoniously makes a beeline for Gertie's lifetime supply of hay.

"Can we help you feed?" I ask hopefully.

"Well, I don't see why not, but I'll warn you—it might end up costing you a chip in one of those pretty blue fingernails," Ben quips.

At this, Thomas lets out an audible snort and covers his face with his hand.

"Nah, they're dip nails—they won't chip," I respond confidently.

"Dip? Is that the same as acrylic?" Ben asks in earnest.

"*Definitely* not," I reply.

The three of us head for the buckets of chicken feed sitting near the coop. Although I seek out the bucket containing the least amount of food, I struggle a bit as I rest the handle on my forearm.

"*What* is she doing? That's not her place!" Leon barks as he makes it over to us.

"The kids here just wanted to help feed the chickens. I didn't think it would hurt anything," Ben replies plainly.

"The weight of the bucket itself looks like it may cause her to tip over, let alone walk around with it," Leon responds haughtily.

My cheeks *must* be growing a darker shade of red by the second. I feel just as embarrassed as I do angry. Sure, *it's heavy*. But I can decide for myself what I can and can't do. I also don't appreciate that he would call *me* out and not Thomas. It's not *his* job to feed the animals either.

"Oh, come on now, Mr. Leon. You know what they say–many hands make light work," Ben protests, picking up a full bucket of feed effortlessly.

Leon scoffs before turning and storming off in a huff.

"Don't worry about him, guys. I don't think he really means half of what he says," Ben interjects, seemingly unbothered.

It doesn't take the three of us long to feed. The task grows easier with every passing minute as my bucket lightens. I can imagine it may be more of a chore in the summer months, but right now the cold is working in our favor. Even still, Ben and Thomas are moving much faster than I am.

As Ben stacks our now-empty buckets, an older blue car can be seen driving towards the house. Although I don't recognize it, there are *a lot* of people who filter in and out of Langley on a daily basis.

"I didn't know your mom was coming by today!" Thomas says, looking over at Ben.

"I didn't either," he replies, waving toward the now-parked car.

A woman wearing an olive-green dress exits her vehicle, smiling in a way that takes up her whole face. I can't help but notice how much she favors Ben, though her skin is a darker hue. Her hair is swept up off her neck. She carries large baskets on each arm, as well as two disposable pans stacked on top of one another in her hands. Thomas and Ben simultaneously hit a stride in order to meet her.

"Why didn't you wait on us to help you, Mom?" Ben asks as he heads for the steps leading into the kitchen, now carrying the baskets.

"Yeah Ms. Cora, wouldn't want to risk dropping all this good food," Thomas adds, carefully holding the silver pans against his chest.

"Oh, I had a feeling that two handsome young men would help a lady out," she replies.

"It's nice to meet you, Ms. Mitchell. I'm…"

"Greer! Yes. I'd recognize you anywhere. You look so much like your aunt," she says with a smile. "I knew both Carl and Cece well... and of course I had the pleasure of getting to know Frank while he was here. All such dear people."

"Yes ma'am. I appreciate your kind words, Ms. Mitchell. And Ben has been so helpful throughout all of this," I add.

"Please, dear. Call me Cora."

I don't know that I've ever met someone with quite the kind, motherly-nature that Cora possesses. It's obvious to me now why Ben has such a generous way about him.

I suppose my aunt was the closest I ever had to a motherly figure. She was kind, and clearly loved Dad and I—but without having any children of her own, I don't know that she ever developed those specific motherly traits. I hope Ben realizes how lucky he is. Though knowing him, I'm confident that he does.

"I've never met two people more generous than your aunt and uncle," she continues as we make it inside the house. "I was so proud when she founded her charity."

"Yes, me too," I respond happily. It's nice to have a chance to talk about Cece—her life; not just her death.

"Of course, I think the most generous thing she ever did was give my son here a job," Cora says, winking at Ben.

As Ben and Thomas begin anxiously removing foil from the disposable tins, Cora heads to a nearby cabinet to fetch serving utensils. The aroma of the various treats fills the air as the boys begin shoveling food on their respective plates.

It isn't long before we are joined by Anne-Marie, as there's no way she could have missed all the commotion. She and I both fix our plates as Cora fills glasses with ice.

"Now, where is Mr. Leon?" Cora asks.

"Oh, he's around here somewhere. I'll take him a plate in a bit if you want, Mom," Ben responds, helping himself to more deviled eggs.

"I do wish you would have let him know I was here so he could join us."

"You know Leon, Mom. Never a fan of a crowd."

Though she seems disappointed in Ben's response, she doesn't press the issue further—for which I'm grateful. I may have a hard time suppressing my feelings toward him should we be in such close quarters.

"And where is your father, Greer?" Cora asks hopefully.

"Owen is back in the office," Anne-Marie interjects. "I didn't want to disturb him, but I'll make sure he eats soon."

***

Nearly an hour has passed since Cora's arrival. Ben and Anne-Marie both returned to work promptly after finishing their meals, with Cora fixing a plate for Ben to deliver to Leon. Thomas and I continue to graze on leftovers. Cora's food is truly like nothing I've ever experienced.

I tell her all about graduating early and starting college courses. I tell her about my plans to apply to art school once I finish my degree.

Although he seems engaged in our conversation, I worry that I'm boring Thomas. It's difficult not to feel a little insecure around him—embarrassed, even. We're friends at Langley—but would we be friends if we went to school together? I sometimes doubt he would notice me at all. Though I'm a social person, I harbor no preconceived notions as to the kind of people I should spend time with. Said plainly—there are no 'cliques' in homeschooling.

"I'd love to see your artwork sometime," Cora says as she finishes restoring the kitchen to its formerly-spotless state.

"Sure," I answer with a grin, though I'm ashamed to admit I haven't worked on anything new since the move... well, since the funerals really.

The conversation wraps up after Thomas and I finally finish nibbling at our smorgasbord of treats and comfort foods. I really hate to see her go, especially since the food and conversation were doing a fine job at distracting me from my concerns over the estate's surly old groundskeeper.

Upon her departure, Thomas and I retreat to the second-floor study. It's a small-*ish* room (compared to the others at least). An entire wall is covered with built-in bookshelves consisting of hundreds of novels, textbooks, and several wire baskets containing magazines which date back to the 1960s. There are two matching leather chairs on the wall opposite the books.

Thomas and I have spent a fair amount of time in here—whether it's in silence (reading and scrolling through our phones), or talking incessantly about topics of little importance to anyone, *even us*. The only reason I prefer to read by the downstairs fireplace when Thomas is absent is because of the second-floor draft which leaves the room bitterly cold. It's as though all warmth tries desperately to flee the room through every crevice, window, and door— no matter how much we turn up the thermostat.

We grab blankets from a large basket which rests near one of the chairs before settling in. Glancing at my phone, I realize it's nearly time for Anne-Marie and Thomas to head home for the day.

It's always a little disheartening as their time of departure draws near. The house feels so empty at night. And it still seems painfully odd being here without Grandpa Frank or Cece. Though I think Dad is way too preoccupied to notice the disconnect.

Admittedly, I wish I could return home. But home isn't there anymore—at least, not as it was. All of our belongings are either at Langley, or were sold via Facebook Marketplace. Though it's a nice place to live, the only thing I really look forward to anymore is my time spent with Thomas. It's a little frustrating that he has such a hold on me—without even trying.

"What'd you think of Cora's cooking? Pretty good, right?" Thomas asks.

"*Really* good," I respond, trying my best to get out of my head and back to reality. Though my head seems at times a safer and more pleasant place to reside.

"Leon was in fine form today, wasn't he? I don't know why he always has to be such a stick in the mud," he says, rolling his eyes.

I nod, though I struggle with a response. *He really has no idea.* Leon has gone way past a 'stick in the mud.' He's deliberately trying to hurt my father, and I need to know *why*.

***

Warm water hits my face as I make a conscious effort to calm my nerves by taking deep, intentional breaths. Thomas and his mother left a while ago, and Langley is now eerily still. Dad went to bed early tonight. He needs the rest.

My former bathroom pales in comparison to the en suite which connects to my new bedroom. As I stand beneath not one, but *two* showerheads, I'm reminded of my time spent at the country club. My friends and I would always hit up the showers to rinse off after spending countless hours in the chlorine-filled swimming pool.

I imagine I'm back there now. Eyes closed. Warm water hitting my face. The smell of berry-scented shampoo as I massage it through my crimson hair– praying the chlorine didn't make any changes to the color. It all feels so far away now.

The water pressure suddenly diminishes drastically. I rush to remove all traces of suds from my hair before it stops altogether. This old house has its quirks, so I'm not too surprised. Wrapping myself in a towel I head toward the door which leads to my bedroom when the lights begin to flicker.

They turn on and off several more times before I've had a chance to dress in my walk-in closet. It's pitch-black outside, and I'm left completely blind every few seconds as the electricity wavers. I hope my eyes can adjust enough for me to make it safely over to my bed, should the lights decide to stay off for good.

I dress quickly in a pair of shorts and loose t-shirt before practically sprinting to my bed. I grab hold of my cell phone to use as a flashlight in case of another outage. Ten minutes pass, and the lights have remained on. Phone in hand, I venture over to my large bedroom window seat which overlooks the property.

The night is still, just as it is inside. The trees outside my window stand motionless. I detect not the slightest hint of wind hitting their branches. I can't imagine *what* could have caused a power outage, but I'm relieved it didn't last long. I certainly wasn't going to wake Dad over it when he's finally getting some rest.

In a corner of the bedroom rests my wooden easel, as well as paints and brushes housed in a cardboard box. Painting has always been my escape. And I could really use an escape right now. Though it's not home, I can appreciate the sheer amount of space I now have to enjoy in my new living quarters.

I'll have ample room in which to create, without fear of getting in anyone's way. I just need the motivation to pick up a brush again. I need to seek out sources of inspiration. Despite its inherent beauty, it's as though all life has been wiped out of Langley within a matter of weeks. It's as though all life has been wiped out of *me* as well.

As I lay my head back on one of the dozens of decorative pillows which line the window seat, it feels as though I'm being swallowed whole by the darkness just outside the glass. The isolation is too much for me. I miss having Grandpa Frank around as my sounding board.

Though I'd never admit it, my relationship with Thomas may be the only thing keeping my head above water at the moment. I'm still unsure of whether or not our chemistry is a result of sheer necessity or genuine connection. My emotions have been a bit blunted lately, so it can be difficult to feel anything at all. I may even have feelings for him which my brain is refusing to allow me to experience.

I look around the room, making a conscious effort not to think of him. My canopy bed dons a silk duvet cover of a delicate shade of lavender. At least a dozen pillows occupy the bed, adding to its look of grandeur. The large footprint of the bed, coordinating side tables, and dresser do little to fill the space of the room.

A small, antique desk rests against the wall–the only piece which is not a part of the bedroom set. It must be at least a hundred years old. I can't help but wonder what the carpenter who built the desk might think should he see that it now supports a modern-day desktop computer. There's something intriguing about mixing ever-changing technology with pieces which have stood the test of time.

The old, wood floor creaks a bit as I swing my legs off the window seat and adjust my position—stuffing a pillow under my arm and peering out at the darkness once again. My eyes have finally adjusted a bit. I can see most of the trees on this side of the property. And I can *just* make out the chicken coop in the distance.

It's easy to detect even the slightest bit of movement against the still of the night. I can't make out who it is at first—*the man stalking around the house*—though I have a pretty good idea. I look on in disbelief as Leon darts toward a first-floor window. It's clear that he does not want to be seen.

Though he typically moves relatively slowly, he is practically jogging from one area to the next. He peers into several windows along the ground floor, whipping his head around periodically to ensure that he hasn't been detected—though I can't imagine *who* he'd be worried about. He's the only person who should be on the property at this time of night, apart from Dad and I. What does he think he's doing!?

Should I have noticed Leon simply walking the property at night (in no rush to make it from Point A to Point B), I could have easily assumed his outing was legitimate. But this is unmistakably different. He does not wish to be seen.

After adjusting the curtain to ensure that my presence is concealed, I hold my breath as I observe him slithering like a deranged serpent along the house. I can feel the adrenaline as it begins to surge through my motionless body. I was frustrated when I learned of Leon's disloyalty, but would he actually try to sabotage us in some way? He and Cece seemed close. Why would he want to hurt us? Hurt the estate? He's worked here for decades!

I lose sight of him as he turns a corner. My heart beats rapidly as I rush to the bedroom next to my own. I catch another glimpse of him through the window as he continues to skulk along the house. I run from room to room, trying to keep up.

Yet again, Leon has stopped to peer into a downstairs window. Meanwhile, I strain my neck in order to keep watch of his movements. My blood runs cold once I realize that he is currently standing outside my father's bedroom.

Without another thought I dash towards the grand staircase. My bare feet pound against the wood flooring with every step. I unlock the front door, trying in vain to steady my breathing. As I make it to the porch, I can hear Leon at the side of the house–likely having heard me by now. It's still pitch black, and my eyes haven't had time to adjust as I run towards my dad's window–ready to confront Leon. I am fully prepared to make a massive scene over his conduct.

I round the corner at a dead sprint. I don't know what I'll say to him. All I know is that he's no friend of ours–and now I've caught him in the act of spying on us.

My eyes adjust quickly to the darkness. I can see the window in which Leon stood just moments earlier. *But no one is there.* The window is locked tightly. Nothing even looks amiss. No tracks on the ground as far as I can tell. I swing my head around, trying to catch a glimpse of him running back to his cottage. But there's nothing. The grounds are still (yet again).

Here I stand in my bare feet and wet hair, chasing after no one. I place my hand on the side of the house, steadying myself. I was sure he was here. How could he have disappeared that quickly?

I'm beginning to question my own sanity as I walk slowly back to the front porch. Is there any way I could have imagined it? Did I nod off at the window seat and then wake up thinking it was real?

As I lock the front door, I turn my head in anticipation of someone lying in wait to grab me from behind. I realize that paranoia is setting in, but still, I walk slowly about the first floor–expecting something to happen. The floors creek beneath my feet, just as they always do. Yet in this moment I wish they could hush themselves just until I have assurance that Leon isn't hiding behind a door with a butcher knife.

I make it to my father's bedroom and slowly turn the doorknob, trying desperately not to wake him. I'm relieved to find him sleeping soundly beneath his comforter, blissfully unaware of the evening's happenings.

I hold onto the railing of the grand staircase as I ascend the steps back to my bedroom. I can't seem to get there fast enough. It's as though they have multiplied since I last climbed them. I finally make it to my doorway when I turn to see a light just down the hallway.

It's one of the other bedrooms. The door is open, and the light is on. A shiver runs up my spine and rests at the base of my skull as I stand paralyzed with fear. I ran from bedroom to bedroom whilst in pursuit of Leon, so it makes sense that I left the doors open in my haste. The other bedroom doors are currently open as well. But I wouldn't have turned a light on. *Would I?* It was all such a blur. I wasn't thinking of anything except catching Leon in the act.

All the boldness and heroism which I experienced as I pursued who I believed to be Leon stalking around our home seems to have now drained from my body. I never take my eyes off the lit bedroom down the hall as I slowly back myself through my own door frame.

I lock the door and check my bathroom and closet for good measure before settling back onto my bed. Cell phone in hand, I close my eyes tightly, trying to convince myself that everything is fine.

The house was locked up before I ran out the front door. I was only outside for a minute, *tops.* And even if someone *had* tried to enter the house, I would have seen them. There would have been no way for them to make it through the front door undetected. I *must* have turned the bedroom light on myself as I dashed from room to room, without thinking.

I grow less confident in what I saw from my bedroom window seat with every passing moment. It *was* very dark outside. And I may very well have been drifting in and out of sleep. But I no longer care to find out. I have zero desire to leave my bedroom again until morning, though I pray the lights will stay on.

The paint supplies (still to be unpacked) grab my attention yet again as I turn to my side and rest my head on one of the pillows lining the headboard.

Maybe I'll paint tomorrow. Perhaps my art was the only thing that ever kept me sane, and now without it I'm slipping into some sort of trauma-induced psychosis before I even have my driver's license. *I'll start painting again tomorrow.*

CHAPTER SIX

Though the tapestries covering my large bedroom window are shut tightly, light still makes its way easily to my eyelids. It can't possibly be morning already, as I'm confident I only fell asleep just minutes ago. The slivers of light do little to coax me out of bed as I cover my face with a pillow and turn to my side opposite the window.

I'm not a fan of those moments after first waking—*the in-between*. When you're not quite sure if you're dreaming or awake. I hate feeling so out of control—not knowing what's real and what is not. It's like I could either hop out of bed and start my day, or perhaps I'll bash the window out of a sinking car and swim my way up to the surface just before I run out of air.

I rarely set an alarm. It was one of the benefits of homeschooling, and now being in college. Online courses don't require a seven-a.m. wake-up call. I pretty much complete my work whenever I feel like it, whether that's two in the afternoon, or three in the morning when I'm having trouble sleeping.

I have no clue what time it is—especially since I don't know when I finally fell asleep. The events of the evening left me on edge as I contemplated my sanity well into the early morning hours. I think I'll try to sleep in a little longer—it's not as though anyone will mind.

Chills cover my arms and legs within a matter of seconds. I jump involuntarily as though I've been hit with a spark of electricity, which has made its way quickly throughout my entire body. I am now wide awake, and painfully aware of my surroundings.

I don't know where it came from–*the scream.*

Was it Anne-Marie? Is she even here yet?

All I do know for sure is that the blood-curdling scream which shocked me into a heightened state of consciousness was *definitely* real. There was no dreaming it. No tricks being played by an anxious mind.

A woman screamed. It may have come from outside the house, but I can't be sure.

I throw the lush comforter from my shaking body as I practically leap out of bed. My bare feet pound once again against the cold floor as I make it to the bottom step of the staircase and towards the door which leads out through the kitchen.

The door sticks as I unlock the deadbolt. Forcing it open, I see Anne-Marie standing alone, several yards from the house. Her hands are clasped tightly to her mouth. She isn't moving–but staring intently into the distance. The blood seems to have drained from her face, and my brain barely registers that my father has now joined me outside–breathing heavily and clearly having been startled from his sleep as well.

Thick fog covers the ground. Though terrified, I turn my head slowly to the right. I take in a slow, shaky breath knowing I'm about to find out *what* could have caused Anne-Marie to inflict such a hellacious noise on the house. I half expect to see my Aunt Cecilia's ghost standing there, based on the terror in her eyes.

As I peer through the fog, I can see that something is scattered along the ground–mostly near the chicken coop. It takes several seconds before I can make sense of the gruesome scene. The bodies of dozens of chickens, pigs, goats, and rabbits litter the dirt in front of me.

The only signs of life are from Langley's only cow, Gertie, and a few chickens running around aimlessly. There are no visible signs of trauma that I can tell. There is no blood. If I didn't know any better, I'd think they were all sleeping–but that's just not the case. Apart from Gertie and the chickens that continue to run smack into one another through the fog, at least fifty deceased animals cover the grounds of the estate.

My father stands just behind me, trying to catch his breath. I hear Ben's voice as he calls out from the front driveway. "What are you all doing standing around for?" he asks in jest, clearly unaware of the grotesque scene in which he's happened upon.

"What the…?" he says before covering his forehead with his hand and turning away. About a minute passes before another word is spoken. I don't think I've ever seen my father this stunned.

"*Owen…*" Anne-Marie gets out before her voice cracks. "What happened to them?"

Dad shakes his head in disbelief, turning to Ben. "Do you have any idea what could have caused this?" he asks, seemingly hopeful that Ben will have some sort of insight.

"I wish I did," Ben responds as he makes his way slowly toward the carnage. He walks gingerly throughout the scene, carefully avoiding the animals. I notice him wince as he passes by the body of a goat he would have cared for just yesterday. "I'm not seeing any signs that it was some kind of predator that got to them. There's no blood; no bite marks."

"We don't have any security cameras on the grounds, do we?" my father asks.

"No. I'm sorry, Owen. I sure wish we did– especially now. Your aunt just couldn't be convinced that we needed them."

Dad crouches down next to several of the bodies, looking them over slowly for any clues as to their cause of death.

"Where is Leon?" he asks abruptly before standing to his feet.

"He told me before I left last night that he wasn't feeling well. Asked if I could manage on my own today," Ben says, unable to hide the uncertainty in his voice.

My father lets out an audible groan before walking back inside the house. "I'll go call the police," he says, nearly slamming the door behind him in frustration.

Ben offers to walk Anne-Marie into the house. Her complexion is still ghostly-white, and she hasn't spoken in several minutes.

The sight of virtually all of Cece's animals deceased on the ground I'd walked just a few hours prior is a lot to process. Thomas knows the area much better than I do; maybe he will have an idea as to what could have happened.

I'm hesitant to share with anyone the events of last night. Could Leon be intentionally trying to push me to the brink? Could he have known I was sitting at my window seat all along? Could he be responsible for these deaths?

No, nobody needs to know about my brush with darkness. At least–not just yet. The last thing I need is for Thomas to think I'm unhinged.

***

It's been about thirty minutes since the police left when I finally spot Thomas letting himself in at the front door–his large backpack slung across his shoulder. Despite waiting all day to talk to him, I almost hate to disrupt his current state of ignorance. Anne-Marie has been cleaning the second floor for quite some time, and Dad let Ben go home early once the police left. So, unless one of them sent him a text, I will have to break the news.

After the police photographed the scene and took statements from my father and Ben, the corpses scattered about the estate were loaded onto the back of a trailer and hauled away. I'm not entirely sure who took care of it. Is that something the police would do? Did my dad call someone? What a terrible job that must have been. I did overhear Ben saying something to Dad about a toxicology report, but I didn't stay outside for long after officers arrived.

I decided to use schoolwork as a distraction, rather than driving myself to the point of jumping off a proverbial cliff obsessing over all that has occurred at the place I now call home.

I finished up the work for my online classes within a couple of hours. I even contemplated jumping ahead a week when the art supplies that remained unused in my bedroom once again grabbed my attention. I know I need to relax, and painting has always worked at calming my anxious mind just as well as anything my pediatrician has prescribed me on and off since I was ten years old.

My easel and paints are resting outside in the dirt, on the side of the house opposite of the crime scene. I have a good start on a small, yellow home sitting off in the distance from Langley. Despite its size and considerable distance away, I could still make out its features pretty well considering there is nothing to disrupt my view of it, only pasture.

I've wondered about the people who live there in that quaint yellow house. I've imagined them to be a family of six, if not more. Mom and Dad both work hard to give their four (or more) children the best life they can. Mom makes dinner every night while the kids work outside with their father.

The small red barn that rests a bit further in the distance than the home has likely been the location of countless lessons from Dad which pertain to vehicle repair, animal care, and lawn maintenance. Though I've invented most of the details of the lives of the family living in the yellow house, I *do* know that they have animals which roam in and out of the barn and along their fence.

After working on my painting for a couple of hours, I decided to store the canvas and paints in the garage for the time being.

Thomas looks me over curiously when he sees that my head is laid back against a living room chair, bottled water in hand. The emotional toll of the day seems to have finally caught up with me.

"Greer?" he asks, an air of confusion in his voice as he pushes hair back from his forehead. "Are you sick?"

"*I'm fine.* I've just been outside for a good while."

I straighten myself up and nervously run my thumb over the rim of my water bottle as he takes a seat.

"Is my mom upstairs?" he asks.

"She is," I respond before taking one last swig of water. "It's… been a day around here."

"Really? What, did Leon get hot under the collar at someone?" he inquires earnestly.

"No. I actually haven't seen him today. Ben said he wasn't feeling his best," I reply, trying not to give too much away with either my facial expression or tone.

"There was an incident. Your mom was the first one to… discover it."

"Discover *what?*" he asks, visibly concerned.

"Apart from Gertie and a few chickens, all of our animals are dead. Your mom found them when she showed up this morning."

A look of confusion engulfs his face as I wait patiently for the inevitable line of questioning to begin.

"They're *dead?* How!?" he asks, the disbelief apparent in his voice. "Was it a predator? Something got to them?"

"We don't think so. They were just scattered along the dirt."

I follow him in silence as he abruptly storms through the kitchen and out the side door. *He must need to see it for himself*–though at this point there's really nothing left to see. A visitor would find nothing amiss–merely a massive, well-kept yard that serves as home to an old cow and a few chickens.

"It just doesn't make sense," he says, breaking the deafening silence which has permeated the grounds since the bodies were removed.

I shake my head in agreement as he turns to face me.

"Why do these things keep happening?" he asks. "Your grandfather, then Cece, and now this… are we cursed or what?"

I shrug, unsure of what to make of it all myself.

"And no one's seen Leon today?" he asks accusingly.

"No," I reply flatly.

"How sick would he have to be to miss that much commotion in his own front yard?"

"Try not to get too worked up, Thomas. We don't know what happened," I plead, though I fully appreciate his frustration.

He scoffs before turning to head back inside.

My stomach turns a bit as I feel him wrap his arm around my back, as though comforting me as we vacate the scene. It's subtle, yet I can feel the adrenaline coursing through my body, just as it did last night whilst in my frantic pursuit of Leon. Or at least–someone I believed to be Leon, though I'm still unsure if it was anyone at all.

His right hand grazes the small of my back before he motions me forward to ascend the concrete steps. It's only now that I realize I've been unintentionally holding my breath for several seconds. I know I probably shouldn't read too much into it, but he's never touched me like that before.

***

My father sat with Anne-Marie on the front porch for over an hour once she'd completed her work for the day. She and Thomas have never stayed over this late. It was nearly eight o'clock before she began fixing dinner for all of us. Thomas and I offered to help, but she and my dad insisted they had it covered. Their desire to be alone wasn't lost on me, though I find myself too drained to really consider why.

Upon his mother's urging, Thomas and I concede to taking a walk outside. We've made an entire loop around the grounds of Langley with hardly a word uttered between us. The crisp night air soothes my skin, gently grazing against my face as we stroll just along the edge of the property. The faux fur lining the interior of my denim jacket keeps me warm, though I can see my breath in front of me as I exhale.

Thomas is wearing a windbreaker type of coat, which features his school mascot adorning the chest pocket. I doubt that it's thick enough to withstand the cold. It seems as though the temperature is dropping with every passing minute. The cold is somehow more unforgiving at Langley than anywhere else, in my opinion—especially after dark. The stillness of the property surrounds us like a veil as we walk—an ever-present reminder of the day's events.

Grandpa Frank and I once found ourselves in the path of a tornado as we traveled home from a beach trip. It was the summer before I started first grade, and Dad was too busy with work to join us. I can still recall the stillness of that night, just before the clouds turned dark and Grandpa sped to the nearest rest stop where we took shelter. It was a menacing quiet, just as it is this evening as Thomas and I walk along in silence. The animals were one of Langley's most endearing attributes—which is now more apparent than ever considering the current state of lifelessness which has overtaken the property.

"Are you about ready to turn back?" Thomas asks.

I can't help but feel a tinge of relief that I haven't fallen deaf within the past half an hour. The silence had become almost too much to endure.

"You must be freezing," I reply sympathetically.

He grins as he places his hand on my shoulder, turning me gently in what I assume to be the direction of the house. I'm glad he seems to know where we are, because I haven't recognized a bit of our surroundings for at least the past ten minutes or so.

"I just don't want *you* catching a cold or something. I'd put my arm around you to stop the shivering but… anyway, I'm sure dinner is ready by now," he says coolly.

That all-too-familiar rush of both excitement and panic nearly causes me to lose all feeling in my already-numb body as I try to imagine what he would have said had he not stopped himself mid-sentence.

"So, what do you think they've been talking about?" I ask, unable to endure a lull in our conversation following his previous statement.

"My best guess is that they didn't want us overhearing them speculate about ol' Leon," he replies, no detectable hesitation whatsoever.

"What? *You* think he could be responsible for what happened?" I ask, careful to keep my cards close to the chest.

"Don't you?" he asks, glancing over his shoulder in my direction.

"*Maybe*… but I don't really know him all that well. I mean, a person would have to be pretty demented to do something like that—*right?*" I ask rhetorically.

"Definitely," he responds, zipping his windbreaker higher in order to cover his neck.

I can finally make out the lights of the house through the trees. Though I've now lost most feeling in my extremities, I find myself wishing our stroll together didn't have to come to an end. It feels somehow as though this is the most intimate time we've ever spent together–despite the countless hours we've been alone previously.

"I'm glad you're here, Greer," he says, just before we've reached the house.

"*Here* as in Langley?"

"Right," he answers with a smirk. "I mean, of course I wish Cece and Frank were still with us, but… I'm glad you're here."

"Me too," I reply. I then bite my inner lip in order to avoid grinning like a fool.

I haven't had a lot of interactions with guys my own age in the past, but I never really felt as though I was missing out on anything. I knew there would be time for those relationships later–*college most likely*. At least, once I'm old enough to go off to school somewhere.

Due mostly to my lack of experience, I don't have a lot of confidence in my ability to read Thomas. What is he like around other girls? Would he want to see me so often if he didn't have to?

The last thing I want is to misinterpret his friendliness as something more if that's not his intention. The risk of embarrassment here feels uncomfortably high. But if nothing else–he *is* someone who knew both Aunt Cece and Grandpa Frank. He's been living through the trauma right along with me–and it really is fortunate that he's around to be both a sounding board and friend.

***

Dinner consists of homemade macaroni and cheese, green beans, and Anne-Marie's signature 'hot-water' cornbread. Upon our arrival she apologized for sending us out in the cold—though in fairness the temperature did seem to drop at a much faster rate than usual. She and Dad must have wrapped up their conversation about whatever it was they needed to discuss in plenty of time before our return, as they seemed to have moved on—laughing and smiling at one another as they filled glasses with ice and ushered us to the dinner table adorned with several tea candles.

Although my father has dated on and off over the years, he never seems to get too serious with anyone. His job has hindered the nurturing of a serious romantic relationship. In fact, I've only been introduced to two of the women he has dated in the past several years. So, naturally, I find myself a bit taken aback at being witness to his interactions with Anne-Marie.

"How do you like the green beans? I told Anne-Marie they were your favorite," Dad asks, grinning warmly at me from across the table. I'm relieved to see him seemingly more relaxed than he has been in quite some time.

"Oh yeah, they're great. Thank you, Anne-Marie," I offer, looking over at her.

"Owen tells me you've shown an interest in cooking," she responds. "Just let me know if you ever want me to show you a thing or two in the kitchen. I'd love to pass my knowledge on to *someone*," she adds, looking squarely at Thomas.

"Mom's a little salty that I'm not interested in learning to cook. *Pun intended*," Thomas interjects with a laugh. Anne-Marie gives him a knowing glance, seemingly conceding to his rejection.

"That'd be great," I respond before grabbing a piece of cornbread.

I'm admittedly relieved that Anne-Marie is opening up to me, as I'm fairly certain she has spoken to me more this evening than every other day since we moved to Langley, *combined*. I can tell that Dad is happy to witness our interaction as well–which makes me wonder if his interest in *her* goes beyond companionship.

CHAPTER SEVEN

The next morning, I watch as Leon saunters around the property, completing his tasks as though nothing untoward had occurred. I wish I could have been there when Ben 'caught him up' after his sick day. I would have waited patiently for a reaction from Leon, or lack thereof. I have a feeling his face gave it all away, though I don't know that Ben is perceptive enough to have noticed. I get the feeling that Ben isn't convinced that Leon is capable of committing such an atrocity as harming animals. Does Leon seriously believe that we wouldn't find his absence yesterday suspicious!?

I wonder if the best way to proceed may be for my father to outright confront Leon, though I know that scenario is unlikely to yield any sort of meaningful resolution. We aren't any closer to the truth of what occurred than we were yesterday. The police promised to call as soon as they had anything to report. From what I've gathered, autopsies will be performed on one or more of the animals to hopefully determine a cause of death.

"Greer? Why aren't you inside? It's freezing out here," Ben says, standing just behind me. I must have zoned out a few minutes back. I'd grown increasingly agitated at the sight of Leon, and shifted my focus to the little house off in the distance.

"I guess I *should* get back inside." My corduroy jacket is simply no match for the bitter chill. "This *has* to be the coldest it's been all winter, huh?" I inquire.

"It sure feels like it," Ben responds as he walks toward the house, carrying an armful of firewood. "This should help," he says, reaching the front porch steps.

"You know I can't turn down a warm fireplace," I reply.

He grins before disappearing into the house. Just as I'm about to follow him, I notice Leon out of the corner of my eye, also carrying firewood. I experience a sudden rush of emotion as we make eye contact, and for a moment my body feels perfectly warm. I now perceive Leon as a threat, whether justified or not.

As he walks past me, I notice a bandage wrapped tightly around his right hand, stained with blood. He wasn't working yesterday. As far as I know he never left his cottage.

"How did you hurt your hand?" I blurt out, seemingly catching Leon off guard with my sudden outburst. I notice him flinch as he turns to face me.

"Fell inside the house last night… cut my hand on the edge of my old coffee table on the way down," he offers, fairly convincingly.

"I'm sorry to hear that. Are you feeling better otherwise? Ben said you were sick."

"Doing just fine now," he says, trying in vain to end the conversation as he continues on in the direction of the main house.

"You must have been shocked when Ben told you what happened yesterday. I was surprised we didn't see you after the police showed up and all. It was quite the commotion," I say, maintaining as much eye contact as he'll allow.

"I heard it," he says, brushing his uncombed hair from his forehead as he balances the stack of firewood in one arm. I then realize that he's clenching an old pocket knife in his fist, pressed up against the wood.

"You must have been pretty sick then… to not check out what was going on," I say, trying to solicit a reaction from him which might give something away.

"Yep, must have been," he responds, unbothered.

There's no detectable change in his voice. His blunted affect is nothing short of bewildering from a man who has expressed emotion so readily in the past–*primarily anger.*

With that, there's nothing left for me to do except allow him to continue on into the house. I then turn as I hear the squeaking of the front gate opening. *It's Anne-Marie.* But–she never comes over on Saturdays.

As she parks, I notice that Thomas is sitting next to her in the passenger seat.

"Good morning, Greer," Anne-Marie says as she hands Thomas his coat, which he gladly accepts before looking my way.

"Are you crazy?" he asks sarcastically. "Why are you just standing out here?"

"Eh, it's not so bad," I respond, trying not to laugh as he throws on his coat in dramatic fashion.

"Well, you do what you want, but I'm getting inside. This is way worse than last night," he says as he strides quickly up the front steps.

Anne-Marie seems to share in my amusement as we watch him retire quickly into the house.

"Are you working today?" I ask.

"Yes. Well, sort of. Your father asked me last night if I would come help re-organize the office," she responds, checking the time on her phone. "I hope we're not too early."

"Don't worry, he's up," I reply, trying my best to ignore the anticipation which is surging inside of me.

Thomas could potentially spend his entire Saturday at the house. It's going to take an exorbitant amount of time for my dad and Anne-Marie to comb through everything in that comically-enormous home office.

It isn't long before Thomas and I settle in next to the living room fireplace. His mom offers up graham crackers, chocolate, and oversized marshmallows on an ornate serving platter, along with two metal roasting sticks. Once she disappears back into the office, we waste no time in creating multi-layer s'mores, all while critiquing one another's roasting skills.

"Are you kidding? Now you're just messing with me," Thomas says sarcastically.

"No, this marshmallow is perfectly roasted! It takes skill to roast without setting them on fire," I retort.

"That crunch you get from the fire is the best part! And I thought you were supposed to be smart," he replies, without even trying to keep a straight face.

"Eh, to each his own, I guess. You have every right to be wrong," I say before taking a gigantic bite of my s'more, resulting in the inevitable mess that follows.

It's about an hour or so before we stop talking long enough to take our plates and what's left of the s'mores ingredients back to the kitchen. As I expected, we haven't seen Anne-Marie again since she served us the tray. It has probably taken them this long to merely evaluate what all needs to be done in there.

As we sit back down in front of the fireplace, I notice that Thomas is considerably closer to me now than he was before. I wish I could know for certain whether it was intentional or not.

I've never thought of myself as a shy person—especially considering I haven't been exposed to nearly the amount of social interaction as most of my peers. But aside from a few celebrity crushes over the years, I've never really had the opportunity to experience the development of romantic feelings for a guy.

My father has always been confident, so I guess you could say I got it 'honestly.' Navigating college at just fifteen years old isn't exactly for the faint of heart (even when it's online). I make friends easily. And although there are, of course, aspects of my physical appearance that I sometimes wish I could change—I know that overall, I'm an attractive girl. I mean, I'm not crazy to think Thomas may have feelings for me, right?

"So, how have you liked living in the big house so far?" Thomas asks. "I mean, excluding all the drama with Leon-the-creep?"

"It's hard to say," I respond, being as honest as I can. "The circumstances surrounding my being here are just so odd that I don't even know how to feel."

He nods sympathetically before moving maybe half an inch closer to me.

"I know that I miss my friends, and our old house. Of course, I miss Cece and my Grandpa Frank most of all. They were really the only close family that Dad and I had, so now it's just us."

"Yeah. It doesn't seem fair. Any of it. But Owen—your dad—he's lucky to have you," he says, looking down as he runs a tassel between his fingertips, which belongs to the rug beneath us.

"There's something I haven't told you. Something I overheard when I was at that nail salon in town," I say, causing him to look up at me with intense curiosity.

"There were two women there. And from what I understand, one of their husbands used to do business with my uncle Carl," I tell him, lowering my voice with every word. "It seems as though our friend Leon has been spreading rumors around town that my father is somehow incapable of handling the business affairs of Langley."

"But, why?" Thomas asks. "Why would he try to sabotage his own employer? And who the heck else would hire him for a manual labor job now at his age?"

"*That* I don't know… it doesn't make sense to me either," I reply with a shrug.

"I'm assuming you haven't told Owen? I can't imagine him keeping Leon on if he knew," he asks.

"No, not yet. He's just got so much on his plate right now. I wanted to somehow try and handle Leon on my own."

"Greer, you've got to tell him," he responds emphatically. "He *needs* to know. I heard him telling my mom how he spends half his time taking phone calls from anxious investors and tenants. And now we know *why*."

I press my hand onto my forehead and shut my eyes, trying to think of how I could break this news gently without giving my poor father a panic attack. My heart begins to pound as Thomas strokes back hair from my face and tucks it gently behind my ear.

I've never been more afraid to open my eyes in my life. His face can't be more than a foot away from mine. *What if he tries to kiss me?* Maybe he's just being affectionate because he knows I'm in desperate need of comforting right now. Maybe this is just his way of being there for me as a friend–but I've never had a guy this close to me before.

I open my eyes slowly, trying my best to read his face before showing any sort of emotion on my own. He looks like he has a lot on his mind as he stares back at me. I grin slightly, as though thanking him for his concern.

"I don't want to tell you what to do…" he says warmly, "it's just my take on the situation. But I think it would be better for Owen to have all the facts. Just… try to have faith that he can handle it. You don't always have to protect everyone, Greer, as much as I know you'd like to. I'm here to support you either way."

At this, he pulls away, breaking eye contact. On one hand I feel relief at the release of tension between us. Yet I also find myself wishing I could somehow bottle that feeling and revisit it whenever I wish. I hate not knowing exactly what he's feeling when it comes to his relationship with me. Though, I wonder if it's the *not knowing* that makes it so exciting.

Every look, every touch between the two of us distracts me—if only momentarily—from the hellish reality I've been living. Nearly everything about my life has changed within an indisputably unreasonable amount of time. Yet here I am, embarrassingly enamored with this person.

A feeling of intense guilt inevitably replaces the rush just moments prior. The future of my aunt's beloved estate is hanging in the balance. I don't need to allow myself a distraction right now. Dozens of animals were just killed—most likely by a mad man on the loose living right in our backyard.

I know that Leon has been spying on us. I also know that he's been trying to undermine the future of Langley. I didn't want to take any of this to my dad before I had proof. But I know that Thomas is right—*I have to tell him.*

"How would you feel about helping me break the news?" I ask hopefully.

Thomas nods in agreement.

THE BIOGRAPHER

"Wow, that must have been a lot for you to process, especially at fifteen," Sadie remarks, looking as though concerned for the girl I used to be.

"Yes... I mean, I suppose it was. Though at the time I was just taking it day by day. I wouldn't say I was really processing any of it. At least not in any sort of meaningful way. It was... *traumatic*," I say hesitantly. "I don't want to make myself out to be a victim."

"You're not," Sadie replies with a kind smile. "It seems like you haven't allowed any of this to dictate the course your life has taken."

"*Thank you*. I suppose that's true. *I haven't.* But... this period of time did change *me* forever. And the memories will never go away," I respond as I stare out a living room window, watching a car drive by in the distance. "Even when I manage to push it far below the surface, I'm betrayed by my dreams. My brain likes to play these scenes on repeat as I sleep, and there's nothing I've been able to do to stop it."

Sadie watches me closely as I speak, never faltering.

CHAPTER EIGHT

It's been about fifteen minutes since my father and Anne-Marie shooed us back into the living room following our conversation about Leon. *I told him everything I knew.* I told him how I'd caught him spying; about the ladies' conversation at the salon. It wasn't easy, yet I feel some sense of relief in not bearing the burden alone anymore.

They were both clearly in shock, yet they hung on my every word without interruption. They waited until I was finished before asking questions–mostly just distinguishing facts from speculation.

I never doubted that my father would trust what I had to say. Although, I wish I didn't have to be the one to say it. No one likes to be the bearer of bad news. And I have a feeling that my words are about to cause drama the likes of which this home has never seen.

"Are you sure? Maybe we should talk to Ben first… get him to go with you," I hear Anne-Marie plead, the concern apparent in her voice.

"No. I'm the one responsible for Langley; it falls on my shoulders alone," my father responds as Thomas and I join them in the kitchen.

Dad is standing next to the door with his hand resting on the doorknob. I notice he's wearing the brown leather jacket that he's owned since the late-1980s–probably the most casual piece of clothing in his closet.

"Well, I get it… I just want you to be careful," Anne-Marie responds before they both turn to face us.

"Are you going to confront Leon?" I ask hesitantly.

"Yes… it has to be done. There's no use in dragging it out. *We need him gone*," Dad responds.

We all nod in agreement.

"Would you like me to go with you, Mr. Owen?" Thomas offers.

"Thank you, Thomas," my father responds, "but I certainly wouldn't want Leon to direct any of his anger towards you. It's best you all wait here."

"Why should *he* be angry? He's the one that's been screwing all of us over since day one," I blurt out before meeting my dad's gaze. "Sorry, I… just be careful. That man is unstable."

"Will do," Dad responds before making his way out the door.

We wait until he's nearly reached Leon's cottage before we have a seat on the steps leading out to the yard. It's a bit of a long walk, so we had plenty of time to throw on our coats and shoes. Thomas and I are sitting next to one another on the same concrete step, with his mother two steps above us. None of us have said a word to one another since Dad left. The air surrounding us is heavy and unforgiving. I find it strangely difficult to inhale a deep breath.

The anticipation is palpable as Dad gets closer and closer to the cottage in the distance. None of us can look away—not even to cough the feral air from our lungs.

Apart from the occasional back-and-forth between my father and Grandpa Frank when he was still alive, I've never seen Dad in a confrontation of any kind. And even his banter with Grandpa was never over anything more serious than dessert or sports.

It doesn't take long before we spot a figure emerging from behind the cottage, just as Dad is knocking on the front door. The seconds seem to pass in slow motion as Leon meets Dad at the front of his home, carrying buckets in each arm. He rests them on the ground as my father approaches him. Leon looks visibly annoyed at Dad's presence already, and there's hardly been enough time for two words to have been exchanged between them.

We all lean forward, listening for their voices in the distance. There is a continuous exchange akin to a ping pong match currently taking place. Though attempts to decipher their words are useless. They are simply too far away.

All we have to go on is body language, and the occasional change in volume of their voices. Although the first minute or two seem to pass by without too much contention, things quickly heat up as we watch Leon throw his hands into the air as he walks furiously away from my father. Yet it doesn't take long before he returns and they're going at it again. I wish I could hear what they're saying.

"Let me know if you want me to head down there, Mom," Thomas says before glancing over at me.

"No. Like Owen said, there's no reason to get you involved. Though if this goes on much longer, I may try to find Ben," she responds.

I can see Anne-Marie's breath with every word due to the bitter cold. Thomas slides closer to me, shivering. Whether it be out of affection or sheer necessity, I don't mind either way.

With my gaze focused intently on the two figures in the distance, I didn't notice at first that Ben is currently strolling along the side of the house, carrying more firewood.

"May I ask what you all are doing?" Ben inquires, looking very amused at the sight of us huddled together in the cold.

Before we have a chance to respond, our attention shifts back to the cabin, where shouting can be heard. My father and Leon are now in an all-out screaming match.

"What the... what's going on with Owen and Leon!?" Ben asks as he slowly lowers the firewood to the ground.

"It's a lot to explain right now," Anne-Marie replies anxiously. "You should just know that Leon is no friend to any of us, and Owen is letting him go."

Ben looks stunned as he catches my gaze.

"It looks to be going about as well as you would expect," Thomas adds.

It's then that we witness Leon quickly making his way over to Dad, grabbing his jacket collar in both hands.

Ben hits a dead sprint towards the two of them. Terror quickly consumes me as I suddenly recall the fact that Leon carries a pocket knife with him at all times. We've all jumped to our feet, though seemingly glued to the staircase in disbelief at the situation unfolding.

Leon releases my father just as Ben reaches them, which allows me a small sense of relief.

Ben inserts himself between the two men, further diffusing the situation. Though he looks angry, my dad turns back–heading towards the big house, as Ben speaks to Leon.

My father's face is uncharacteristically red, and his knuckles are clenched tightly as we meet him in the yard.

"I told him he needs to be off the property by tomorrow," Dad manages to get out before burying his head in his hands. I've never seen him so angry. I can tell he's trying desperately to calm himself, though I imagine the adrenaline rush is far from subsiding.

"It looked like you showed a lot of restraint just now, Owen," Anne-Marie says reassuringly.

"Well, I'm just glad Ben showed up. I don't think I'd be feeling too good about myself if I'd hit an old man," Dad replies.

I can see the devastation in his eyes, but know that there's nothing to be said in this moment that would help. He just needs some space to clear his head and wind down.

"Anne-Marie, would you mind taking him for a drive? I'm sure Ben can handle things from here," I suggest.

"That's not a bad idea," Dad interjects, walking quickly to the front of the house.

"Of course. Just let me grab my purse inside," Anne-Marie replies, placing her hand on my shoulder as she passes. "But I want you two to stay inside, okay?"

"Yes, ma'am," Thomas and I respond in unison.

As I ease into the comfort of my chair next to the living room fireplace, Thomas grabs more wood for the dwindling flame. Although I know logically it was the right thing to do, I can't help but feel a sense of guilt that *my* words caused all of this. A man lost his job today, one that he'd held for decades. How would Aunt Cece feel about this if she were alive? She always seemed fond of Leon, though it's (admittedly) hard to imagine *why*.

"How are you holding up?" Thomas asks as he adds wood to the crackling fire.

"Fine I guess," I respond, though not even sure myself.

"It's not your fault, Greer," he says plainly.

"I just feel like we're letting Cece down by not keeping Langley exactly the way she left it. Why *does* Leon hate us so much?"

"He's just a grumpy old man, Greer. He's set in his ways, and couldn't adjust after your aunt died. But that's on him, not you or Owen," he offers. Thomas may be more mature than I've given him credit for. He can be pretty insightful when it counts.

"But where will he go now? This has been his home for so long," I reply, trying to fight off tears. "It doesn't excuse anything, but I know he's still grieving. And grief can affect a person in a lot of different ways."

I gaze fixedly at the fireplace which is now roaring nicely, with no signs of letting up. The ornate mantle frames the scene as the flames ebb and flow. I feel its warmth cover me like a blanket, thinking of how many times Cece and Uncle Carl must have sat in front of this very fireplace, discussing their life together; thinking of all they had built and all they had left to do.

Even after Carl passed, I bet Cece sat here thinking of him. And now here I am, thinking of *her*, and of Grandpa Frank.

I'm afraid to look over at Thomas, as the sight of the crackling fire calms my nerves. I wish I had memories of my mother, like I do of Cece and Grandpa. But all I've ever had are photographs of her stashed away in various drawers around the house. I recall that as a child I would clutch tightly onto her antique pearls and scarves, which she wore tied in her hair.

I even found a bottle of perfume in a compartment of her old suitcase once. I'd use it to spray my pillowcase ever so slightly, praying she'd somehow find me in my dreams. *She never did.* And I never told my father about the perfume. I didn't want to cause him further pain, especially since he likely has specific memories tied to the scent, whereas I do not.

"I'm sorry you've lost so many people in your life, Greer. *I really am,*" Thomas says softly. When I finally look over at him, I can sense that he's been watching me sit here quietly for a while. Perhaps just waiting patiently for me to make my way out of the weeds of my thoughts, *afraid to say the wrong thing.*

"Thank you… *for caring.* It helps," I respond, managing to look him in the eyes as I speak.

"Could you tell me about your mother?" he asks.

I can only assume that he can sense the sorrow radiating from every fiber of my being. It's as though he doesn't want me to sit here alone with it anymore. Like he wants to share in the burden.

"She had long, red hair; deep green eyes. She was… *enchanting.* At least, that's what Dad and Grandpa Frank always said. And from the photos I have of her, I think they were right." Thomas looks at me as though I might break. "But she passed well before I could even walk. Grief is… complicated, especially when grieving someone you never really knew."

Thomas nods in agreement as he adds another piece of wood to the fireplace.

"But then to lose Frank and Cece… it doesn't seem fair," he says sympathetically. "I mean, I get that Leon lost a friend, but other people have it much worse. *Like you and your dad.*"

The kitchen door swings open. The frigid wind creeps inside as well, despite how quickly Ben shut the door behind him. It's as if the cold is trying in vain to beat down the walls of the estate–howling and carrying on as we do our best to remain warm.

"Greer?" Ben calls out.

"In here."

"Hey, are you two okay?" he asks as he joins us in the living room.

"I'd expect we're doing better than you," Thomas remarks. "Have you been with Leon all this time?"

Ben nods his head before taking a seat next to Thomas. "I was just trying to talk him off the ledge. You know how he can be."

It's apparent how drained he is as he sits slumped over with his hand pressed against his cheek.

"I'm sorry you had to get involved," I say, turning to face him.

"Could the two of you please tell me what's going on?" Ben asks. "All I got out of Leon was some incoherent ramblings as he was throwing some clothes into a suitcase."

I go on to explain all that transpired earlier in the day. *All that I've personally seen and heard.* And why Dad felt he had no choice but to let Leon go. Ben listens attentively, nodding his head occasionally. As I tell him all about the night I caught Leon snooping around the house, part of me hopes he doesn't think I'm crazy. He *does* know Leon a lot better than he knows me.

Ben remains quiet for several seconds, directing his gaze at the roaring fire. I can tell he wants to be especially careful with his words–he's smart like that. He's the type to actually think before he speaks.

"Leon is a pain. There's no denying it… but I never pegged him as disloyal. I'm sorry to hear he's been bad-mouthing your father," Ben says, shaking his head in disbelief. "Even if he didn't care for Owen… I thought his dedication to your aunt would be enough to keep him grounded. I don't mean for this to sound like an excuse, but he's been out of his mind since Cece died. *Heartbroken.* To tell you the truth, I've worried that something inside him snapped."

"The working-class doesn't have the luxury of *snapping*," Thomas retorts. "My mom always says that breakdowns are only for the rich."

"Well, she's right about that," Ben replies, "if the working man loses his mind, he'll be out on the street within weeks."

I feel like Ben is holding something back. Like he's trying to decide whether or not we can be trusted to hear what he has to say.

"What is it?" I ask, hoping to share in whatever it is that's clearly troubling him.

"Okay…" he replies hesitantly, "there's something about Leon that you should know."

He takes a deep breath before continuing. Thomas and I wait patiently in silence, as though to avoid saying anything which might cause him to change his mind.

"I had to help Leon move some furniture in his house a while back. It was the first and only time he's invited me inside," Ben says, still a bit guarded.

It feels like his words are hitting me in the gut one by one. What did he see!? A dead body? A bloody axe? A list of everyone who has wronged him?

"I'd asked to use the restroom while there," Ben continues. "Leon's bedroom door was open when I passed by. I honestly wasn't trying to look, but you just couldn't miss it."

"Miss *what?*" Thomas asks.

"A photo," Ben says reluctantly. "There was a framed photo right on his nightstand... of Mrs. Cecilia."

"*Cece*!? What do you mean?" I ask, despite the fact that there is no need for clarification.

"Why would he want a framed picture of his boss to wake up to every morning?" Thomas asks, seemingly oblivious as to the implication.

"Other than an old alarm clock, it was the only thing sitting on the bedside table," Ben adds.

"Did Leon have... *feelings*... for Cece?" I ask in disbelief. "But... she was married! To Uncle Carl! Leon and Carl were friends."

"Oh, I know," Ben replies, shaking his head. "I never told anyone, of course. But from then on, I paid a heck of a lot more attention to how he would act around her."

"And?" I ask.

"And... Leon is a strange guy. But I think he loved her. I mean, he was just different when around her. Maybe it was infatuation; I really couldn't tell you," Ben says with a shrug of his shoulders.

Thomas looks over at me with unadulterated bewilderment in his eyes.

"So, was Leon trying to break up the marriage of his best friend and his wife? *DID* they actually get together!?" Thomas asks, exasperated.

"I've told you everything I know," Ben replies, "I never witnessed anything that made me think she felt the same... but I don't know."

I can't seem to wrap my head around the idea that Leon may have been pining away for my Aunt Cece all these years. Should I be ticked off about this? Who the hell does he think he is? Cece was a married woman! And his employer! Did he confess his feelings for her once Uncle Carl died? Did she reject him?

"I didn't think that old codger *liked* anyone, let alone *love*," Thomas interjects.

"Maybe he really did lose his mind after the car wreck. *After she died,*" I offer, before sitting with my thoughts. Luckily, it seems as though Ben and Thomas both need some time to think as well.

CHAPTER NINE

Our monstrous home seems quieter than ever before. It's as though it, too, is still reeling from the bit of information Ben shared with us earlier in the day. In a way, it feels like Leon's secret is one of those things that should have never been known to anyone but him. Like it's something intended to be taken to the grave, and nowhere else.

We've all experienced both thoughts and emotions that will never see the light of day. We don't write them down. We don't tell a soul. These are the thoughts that we will never release from their prison known as the human mind.

It feels wrong to discuss Leon's deepest secret amongst ourselves, as we did earlier in the day. Perhaps Thomas and Ben both felt the same, because they moved on from the topic quickly, and we all went about our day as normally as possible.

While Ben went back to work, Thomas and I waited for our parents to return home from their drive, snacking on popcorn that we'd mixed with chocolate chips. Even in the midst of all the turmoil at the estate, I find myself enjoying every uninterrupted minute I get to spend with him.

"It's good, right?" Thomas asks.

The mix of salty popcorn with the sweetness of milk chocolate has caused me to stuff an embarrassingly large portion size into my mouth. As a result, I can only nod as he looks up at my undoubtedly chipmunk-like face.

"Mom and I make this all the time," he continues.

"It's *really* good. I'm surprised I've never thought of it before. Seems so obvious," I reply, taking a sip of ice water to ensure no popcorn remnants remain clinging to my teeth. "How do you think Leon's going to be able to pack up his whole cottage before tomorrow?" I ask as I peer out the window of one of the many guest rooms.

This particular guest room boasts a large antique bed with a blue, silk comforter folded neatly near the footboard. The en suite bathroom includes white marble floors and ornate gold mirrors hanging above each of the two sinks.

Thomas and I have been sitting near one of the bedroom's two grand windows for the better part of an hour. The matching accent chairs (in which we've made ourselves comfortable) seem as though they would have fit in nicely in a first-class stateroom or lounge onboard the maiden voyage of the Titanic.

We've never before spent time in this particular room, but for today it offers us one key feature—the best view of Leon's cabin from inside Langley. The heavy drapes only graze over the sides of the window, leaving a wide-open view of the back of the estate.

We have kept an unabashedly close watch over Leon's dwelling—waiting for something to happen. So far, he has remained inside, though we've seen his shadow pass by a window at least two dozen times.

"I would think Ben will help him out. I kind of doubt any of the furniture belongs to Leon anyway. Knowing your aunt, she was probably the one to furnish it," Thomas replies.

I nod, looking out once again at the small cottage in the distance, smoke rising steadily from the chimney.

"I'm glad he's leaving," I say, slinking back into my upholstered armchair.

"So am I," Thomas responds. "The man hasn't had to pay rent in over twenty years. He has no children. Hardly ever leaves the property. He should have plenty of money to retire with."

"Yes, though retirement money isn't going to do him much good if he ends up in jail for killing our animals," I retort, agitated at the thought.

"That's true, but I think it will be tough to prove," he offers with a frown.

"Well, at least we won't have to see him anymore. No matter what happens."

Thomas nods in agreement as he polishes off the last remaining chocolate chips that have sunk down to the bottom of the popcorn bowl.

The sound of the front door creaking open can be heard just before a loud crash. The cold wind is barreling its way inside like an unwanted houseguest–unrelenting as it asserts its dominance throughout most of the first floor. Thomas and I rush hurriedly downstairs.

My father pushes the heavy door shut as Anne-Marie scrambles to pull an overturned coat rack upright.

"Gracious!" she exclaims, gathering up coats and an umbrella from the floor.

"Did the door get away from you guys?" Thomas quips.

"Sure did," my father replies, taking several coats off Anne-Marie's hands.

"How was the drive?" I ask hopefully.

"It was just what I needed," he responds, directing a quick glance back at Anne-Marie.

Thomas seems oblivious to their unspoken exchange.

"It's hard *not* to get cooled off while out in *this* weather!" Thomas remarks jokingly.

"I can't argue with that," my father answers, hugging my neck as he passes. "Oh Greer, Anne-Marie and I were talking about you on our drive. I realized you have your day with Mrs. Paisley tomorrow. With everything going on, it sure did slip my mind."

"Mine too," I respond. "Do you think we should cancel it?"

"No, I think it would be good for you to get out of the house," he says.

Mrs. Paisley was a lifelong friend of my Grandpa Frank. After my mother passed, she took an interest in me—the motherless little girl with a fondness for tea parties and adult conversation. By the time I was five, I can recall waiting by the living room window for her to pull into our driveway the first Sunday of each month.

She drove a black Jaguar and always smelled of Chanel No.5.

I enjoyed her company, and Grandpa loved to see the two of us together. He worried about me growing up without another female in our household.

"Do you have a dress for The Glenview?" Dad asks warmly.

"You know I have a closet full," I reply as we all head into the kitchen.

"It's *freezing* outside. I don't think you have a heavy coat nice enough to wear to the tea room."

"Dad, I'll just take it off as soon as we sit down. I'm sure I have a coat that's good enough for that."

"There's a really nice clothing boutique in the town square," Anne-Marie adds. "They're always posting the most beautiful coats on their Facebook Page."

Her comment was all it took for my father to insist I head there immediately before they closed for the day. He's always been overly concerned with what I wear. He never wanted anyone to think he wasn't taking care of me just as well as a mother would. *I didn't either.* And as a result, I think we've both overcompensated a bit. I don't know any other girls my age who own more pairs of panty hose and 'business casual' dresses than they do yoga pants.

Though Dad initially offered to drive me, Anne-Marie quickly volunteered Thomas. As he and I both bemoaned the idea of getting out in the bitter cold, it became apparent that neither Anne-Marie nor Owen would be taking 'no' for an answer.

As he shuts the front door behind us, I wonder if
Thomas picked up on his mother's apparent desire to be,
yet again, alone with my very single father. The herculean
wind jolts me back to the present moment as it smacks
me repeatedly in the face. Thomas runs ahead of me,
frantically unlocking his car. As I reach the passenger-
side, he is already sitting in the driver's seat, his arm
stretched over the middle console in order to prop open
my door.

As I slide into the seat next to him, I'm relieved to
find respite from the elements as the vehicle slowly
warms to a comfortable temperature. We remain idle for
several minutes as the windshield wipers scrape off bits of
ice and snow from our field of vision.

"Has Ben ever told you about Mr. Ronald?"
Thomas asks as we proceed down the driveway.

"Mr. Ronald?"

"He and his wife own the only other house on
this street," he continues.

"I've wondered who lives there. In my mind it
was an eccentric oil and gas heiress named Muffy," I
reply, glancing over at him.

He grins. "No ma'am. *It's Mr. Ronald.* He owns
real estate."

Mr. Ronald's home appears to be even larger than
Langley, though it's difficult to tell. The home sits back
on the property—mostly concealed by massive trees. An
automatic gate covers the entrance to the driveway, with
at least an eight-foot-tall fence extending along the entire

property line. Security cameras perch atop the gate, as well as along the fencing.

"It's almost like a compound, isn't it?" Thomas adds. "I've met him a few times."

"Do you know if Cece knew them very well? *He and his wife,*" I ask, genuinely curious as to their relationship.

"As far as I could tell they were friendly. Of course, they've been neighbors forever… the only neighbors either had," he replies.

It's easy to feel a bit isolated while living at Langley. I wonder if Mr. Ronald and his wife used to have a house full of children before they all grew up and moved away. I expect the silence of a house that massive would be deafening if you're not accustomed to it. Of course, Carl and Cece lived in a home littered with empty bedrooms, never knowing anything different.

"So, I'm taking you to Fireflies, right?" Thomas inquires. I feel certain I'd be happy to go just about anywhere with him. He's not a bad looking chauffeur.

"Is that what it's called?" I ask as I take in the scenery.

"I've heard some of the girls at school talking about it; a lot of them work there. It has kind of a cult-following in our town."

"A *boutique?*" I ask, confused.

"It's like a status symbol," he adds with a grin.

"Well, fireflies *are* pretty… *and elusive.* I guess there are worse names for a boutique," I respond as he pulls the car into a large, mostly-empty parking lot lined with shops. I'd imagine that most shoppers are smart enough to stay home during *this* kind of weather.

"What do you mean?" Thomas asks curiously.

"I mean, I like the name—who doesn't like lightning bugs?"

"But..." he presses, furrowing his brow in amusement.

"But... *they're beautiful.* They burn brightly, just like any girl would want to. *But,* the burn is short lived. It isn't constant. It's not something they can maintain."

Thomas looks at me as though he's trying to solve a puzzle—one with no less than two-hundred pieces consisting of only a blue sky. No variation in color. Nothing to go on but the shapes of the pieces themselves.

"I guess what I'm trying to say is that fireflies are pretty but... *flashy.* Probably not unlike the clothes hanging in that store," I continue.

He stares at me a moment longer—most likely contemplating an appropriate response to whatever nonsense I just spewed.

"I don't think I've ever heard a dissenting opinion on... lightning bugs. Or any insect for that matter," Thomas says grinning. "So, what would *you* name a clothing store?"

I'm pretty sure the only way to save this conversation is to make it seem as though it was always leading up to a predetermined punchline.

"Hmm, how about… *Glowing Click Beetles*? Unlike fireflies, they emit a *constant* glow. No flashing," I respond, hoping this won't be the first and *last* outing the two of us ever have together.

I can tell he's trying not to laugh.

"Yeah, I could see that," he says. "In a few years' time, they'll be asking celebs on the red carpet… *who are you wearing?*"

"Glowing Click Beetles!" we respond in unison.

***

We only spent about ten minutes in Fireflies. I just looked for something my dad would deem fancy enough for the Glenview Tea Room—and fancy enough for Mrs. Paisley. I spotted the white, faux fur coat displayed on a mannequin, accenting a beaded cocktail dress beneath it.

It really is beautiful, and I've always found it mostly sweet that my father wants to ensure I'm always presentable. And although the coat is certainly *flashy*—my father's gesture comes from a good place, and I want to make him happy. Though I'll admit, it was hard to see it that way when I was a six-year-old with a solid rotation of panty hose and half-inch pumps to be paired with mostly lace dresses.

"Is there anywhere else you'd like to go before we head back?" Thomas asks, pulling slowly back onto the main road.

A part of me wants to get back to Langley as soon as possible, for fear of missing any Leon-related incidents. Although, this is the first time I've ever been driven around by a boy. And I can't say I mind it.

"Where do *you* usually go?" I ask, hoping to leave the decision up to him.

"Langley... and school," he quips. "Of course, there's also the doughnut shop. They have really good hot chocolate too."

It only takes us about five minutes to arrive, even with Thomas driving fifteen miles under the speed limit due to ice. The parking lot is a lot fuller than I was expecting. I notice that a lot of the vehicles are sporting decals in support of the local high school.

The car has barely had enough time to warm up when Thomas pulls into a parking spot. I notice that the wind has let up a good bit since we left the house, which makes the walk into the eatery a bit more tolerable.

The interior is decorated in fun retro colors and patterns, though it's a bit unclear if the owners were going for an 80s or 90s motif. Nearly all of the patrons appear to be of high school age. Several seem as though they recognize Thomas immediately.

I've assumed Thomas to be a popular student— beloved by both peers and staff. Though I used to interpret some of his commentary as arrogance, I've come to realize that he, in fact, doesn't take himself too seriously. He tries very hard to put everyone around him at ease, even at the risk of looking foolish himself.

I've always known that our relationship (up until this point) has existed in a vacuum. I have no real competition for his attention. I haven't witnessed his interactions with other girls, and am therefore unaware of whether or not our friendship is anything more. Although curious, I'm a bit terrified his general demeanor will prove to be the same with every other girl as it is with me.

"Hey man, how's it going?" I hear from across the room. It's a boy nearly as tall as Thomas, with dark brown hair, and wearing a green Northface jacket.

Thomas and I share a quick glance before he leads me over to where the boy and several of his friends are standing. I notice that a group of girls are also venturing over from the front counter. They carry with them small paper bags, presumably filled with doughnuts.

Thomas greets his friends before turning to face me.

"This is Greer Tipton. She and her dad live at Langley Estates now," he says before placing his hand gently on my back.

This sudden gesture somehow results in a rush of nerves that weren't present when we first walked in. I may be social on the surface, but meeting friends of Thomas isn't something I was expecting to do today. And of course, the drama at the house has left me a bit on edge to begin with.

They all take turns introducing themselves as the girls join the group. A tall brunette named Padgett makes me feel a bit more at ease due to her friendly demeanor. The girls next to her are both blonde, and much shorter than she is.

"Would you like some hot chocolate, Greer?" Thomas asks while walking slowly towards the front counter. It seems as though he wants me to stay put while he orders, and I'd like to avoid coming across as needy by following after him.

"Sure," I respond, my voice cracking slightly.

"Where do you go to school?" one of Padgett's friends asks once Thomas is out of earshot.

"Well, I'm… Uhh, actually in college. I'm taking online courses right now for my Bachelor's degree."

They are all clearly very surprised by my answer, as evidenced by their facial expressions.

The guy wearing a Northface jacket–who introduced himself earlier as Noah–seems to be the leader of the friend group, as he quickly begins asking follow-up questions in rapid succession before anyone else has a chance.

Had I not already graduated from high school, I would have been a freshman this year (based on age). I've gathered through our conversation that, like Thomas, Noah and the others are all juniors.

Thomas returns several minutes later and hands me a warm to-go cup and paper bag. As I turn back towards the group, I recognize a look of disappointment on Padgett's face.

"You're not staying?" she asks him, glancing over at me as well.

"No, I need to get Greer home before her father sends a search party," he responds jokingly.

After saying our goodbyes, Thomas and I take a moment at a nearby table to gather ourselves before stepping back out into the below-freezing temperatures. He stuffs his own paper bag into one of his jacket pockets before fetching his car keys from another. Just as we are ready to head out the door, I hear Padgett call his name from across the room.

"Hey, wait up," she says before hurrying over, leaving her friends behind. *She seems nervous.* Not at all the same as she was before.

"Could I speak to you privately for just a minute?" she asks, looking squarely at Thomas. Though she does take a moment to acknowledge my presence as well.

"Uhh… sure. I mean, *yeah*," he responds, clearly taken a bit off guard.

I wait by the door until Thomas returns a few minutes later.

"You ready?" he asks warmly.

***

Neither one of us said much on the ride back. I thanked him for the hot chocolate and doughnuts, which were gone by the time we made it to Langley. With the sun now set, the temperature was noticeably cooler as we both jogged toward the front porch.

Dad and Anne-Marie were eager to see the coat I purchased from Fireflies. Though my father seemed very pleased with my selection, he quickly excused himself to retire once again to his office, with Anne-Marie soon following. I wonder how late they're planning on working.

"How about a movie?" Thomas asks, grabbing the television remote off the comfortable leather couch housed in the keeping room, just off the kitchen.

"Sure," I respond, trying my best to get his interaction with Padgett off my mind.

"Your friends were nice," I say, taking a seat at one end of the couch.

Thomas grabs a blanket from a hope chest next to the window and tosses it to me. He then makes himself comfortable on the couch as well–far enough away that we each have a little room to stretch out, but close enough that we can share the blanket.

"Yeah. They're nice guys," he says casually.

"So… how well do you know the girls that were with them?" I ask, hating myself a little bit more with every passing word.

"I've known Padgett for a while. But I think the other two only transferred to our school maybe freshman year."

I hate that I'm feeling jealous of a girl I don't even know. What could she have needed to talk to him about that I couldn't hear? I know that it's none of my business–and I'm pretty sure if I ask him what was said I may as well stick a fork in our relationship.

She was nice. And she was tall. She was just… undeniably pretty. Not to mention, she's older than I am. Thomas has every right to like her. In fact, he'd probably be crazy if he didn't. And it's not as though he has ever explicitly expressed interest in *me*.

"What is it?" he asks.

The lights are all off in the informal living room, apart from a glow radiating from the television. There is also a single light on just above the sink in the kitchen. The wind seems to have picked back up again–howling loudly as it hits the siding of the house.

In the distance, there is a lonely cottage–lights still on. It's hard *not* to wonder how Leon is doing, packing up his entire life. Everything feels so uncertain, and even a little scary. The only familiarity I have right now is the ease and comfort that comes with hanging out with a friend. And yet–even *that* feels different tonight.

"What's wrong?" he asks, now leaning slightly towards me.

"I don't know how to… *how to explain*," I reply honestly.

"I'm sorry if that thing with Padgett made you feel uncomfortable," he offers.

"Oh… no, it's okay. I mean… you can talk to anyone you want–*obviously*."

It seems like Thomas is (yet again) trying to prevent himself from laughing as he inches closer to me.

"Would you like to know what she wanted to talk to me about?" he asks.

"You don't have to tell me," I respond, embarrassed.

"I don't want you to worry about it. Though, I guess I *was* kind of hoping to spare you."

"Spare *me*?" I ask, growing increasingly anxious.

"Padgett's father was good friends with Carl. And I think they did some business together, too. It seems as though Leon's rumors are really making the rounds," he says with a shrug.

"She… was asking you about… *what*—the estate? My dad?"

"*Essentially*. She said her parents had been talking about it, and she knows my mom works here. So, she just wanted to get some information to take back to them I suppose. You know—your aunt and uncle, Langley, the business side of it—they're all kind of a big deal in this town."

"That's what I've been told," I respond, understanding now why he didn't immediately offer to tell me what that awkward interaction with Padgett was all about.

"Don't worry—I just told her that from what I can tell, Mr. Owen is doing really well handling the estate—especially considering it was all so sudden. Your Grandpa had been preparing for a long time to take over. Your father didn't have that luxury."

"I'm sorry you're having to deal with all of this, just because of your association with us," I reply earnestly.

"Greer, *stop*. It's not a big deal. Especially compared to the way your whole life has been uprooted."

The light emitting from the television brushes gently against the side of his face. I've been lying to myself for such a long time–pretending I didn't have feelings for him. All of the emotions I've tried to suppress are now bubbling to the surface, desperate to be acknowledged.

I can't think of a single thing to say to him as we remain turned toward one another. There is nothing but silence between the two of us, yet it's not an uncomfortable silence. It feels as though we have hit some sort of point of no return. There's just no way that we can simply skim over this moment and continue on as if nothing happened.

It's exciting, yet also terrifying. I half expect him to lean in at any moment to kiss me. Yet, the other half of me is certain he will try to let me down gently, telling me that he values our friendship and that he enjoys the time we spend together.

He moves his right hand slowly toward me on the couch. I feel a twinge of embarrassment that my body covers in chills just as he touches my arm. We are now sitting mere inches from one another, still sharing a blanket.

The wind outside is joined by the sudden thud of rainfall hitting the roof with impressive force. I feel a cold chill creeping slowly up my back and making its way to my neck. The keeping room is home to only one old window, which extends from the baseboard to the ceiling. Though it seems impenetrable, I wonder if the persistent wind has finally discovered a tiny sliver of space in which to pass through—allowing it to invade our warm living room.

Thomas uses the back of his hand to graze over my cheek, then gently grabs the back of my neck. My long, red hair falls slightly in front of my face, but he tucks it back behind my ear before I have a chance to react.

"Are you getting cold?" he asks under his breath.

"*No.*"

At this, I feel the tug of his hand on my neck as he pulls me in close. The small amount of light present in the room dissipates. My eyes are now closed tightly. I feel the warmth of his breath on my skin as the gap between us becomes nonexistent.

His lips meet mine with a gentleness consistent with every touch we've shared between us thus far. Moments later, I wrap my arms around his neck and pull myself in closer.

CHAPTER TEN

I never really had what I would consider to be a traditional childhood. My (slightly unconventional) little family consisting of only myself, my father, and grandfather has always been more than enough for me. But I never saw myself as being any different from Dad or Grandpa Frank. I've always been an adult, just waiting for my body to catch up.

It was only natural that I be allowed the freedom to determine my own sleep schedule from a very young age. No one has ever had to look over my shoulder or fuss about things like bedtime, brushing my teeth, or finishing schoolwork in a timely manner. In fact, the services of my alarm clock were typically required just once per month.

Sundays spent with Mrs. Paisley were one such occasion that required an early wake-up call. It was always the same–we'd attend the sunrise service at her church, then off to the Glenview Tea Room for warm drinks and cold finger sandwiches. Mrs. Paisley has always been good company. And like my dad and grandfather, she never treated me as though she was babysitting. It has always been more like two old friends catching up.

It was especially difficult adhering to a specific wake-up time this morning. My dad and Anne-Marie stayed up late organizing the office, though I'd expect it will take at least a week or so to make sense of it all. But the room is now at least a little less panic-inducing.

Thomas and I both remained pretty subdued after we kissed. He kept one arm wrapped around me as I laid my head on his shoulder. It wasn't long after that Anne-Marie was ready to head home. Of course, we were quick to put some distance between us on the couch as soon as we heard the office door opening.

Upon their departure, I quickly retired to my room. The cool sheets on my welcoming bed felt particularly soothing against my skin. Unfortunately, I found it impossible to calm my mind long enough to fall asleep.

One thing I knew for certain was that I felt happier than I had in a long time. Giddy, even. And I must have passed out eventually, because the insufferable sound of my alarm this morning left me feeling agitated at the sudden intrusion on my sleep.

After finishing up with my hair and makeup I make my way hurriedly towards the guest bedroom with the clearest view of Leon's cottage. I didn't think anything could have taken my mind off the fact that Leon is due to move off the property today, yet the new development in my relationship with Thomas certainly gave it a run for its money.

The cottage in the distance looks just as it always has–modest, unassuming, still. The lights are all on inside. I wonder if Leon is up early as well, or if he had to work all night in order to finish packing up by this morning.

"Greer? Are you up?" I'm surprised to hear Dad's voice, as I felt certain he would sleep in this morning after all the work he and Anne-Marie put in yesterday.

"Yes. I'll be right there," I reply, taking one last look at the cabin.

I find him clutching his favorite mug in the kitchen. He looks comfortable, still wearing his robe and slippers.

"Coffee?" he asks.

"No, I think I'll wait to have some tea after church this morning."

"Well, that's actually why I'm up… Mrs. Paisley is sick. She called to let me know she's not going to be able to pick you up today. She said to tell you how sorry she is… but she can't even get out of bed right now," he says. I can tell he's disappointed it's not going to happen for me today.

"Oh, goodness. Well, that's okay. I just hope it's not anything too serious," I respond, trying to mask my own dismay at the turn of events.

"And you look so pretty, too," Dad interjects.

"Thank you. I was actually looking forward to trying out my new coat today," I say with a grin.

"I know it," he replies. "You would have been the talk of the tea room."

A sudden knock at the side door interrupts our conversation. It's still dark outside. Dad seems just as confused as I am. Who could possibly be here this early? The sun seems nowhere near ready to rise for the day, despite the commotion at the house.

Dad pulls back the curtain which covers a small window just above the kitchen sink and peeks out. When he opens the door, I'm surprised to see Ben and his mother, Cora, standing there.

"Good morning! I'm glad to see you two were already up," Ben says, glancing over at me. "You look to be in your Sunday best, Greer."

"Why don't you come on inside?" my father asks, holding the screen door open.

"I'm sorry to show up like this, Mr. Owen. I just saw that the kitchen light was on," Ben says as we all take a seat. "I tried to call last night, but I know you and Anne-Marie were getting a lot done in the office, right?"

"Yes. *I'm sorry*. I didn't see you'd called until it was way too late to return it," Dad says.

"Well, Leon got a hold of me yesterday evening. He asked if I would get here early this morning with a trailer and help him move his stuff... and Mom offered to come along and assist," Ben responds, looking over at Cora.

"I don't know how much help I'll be, but nonetheless..." Cora says warmly. "My, Greer, you sure do look beautiful this morning. Where are you off to?"

I tell them about my friend, Mrs. Paisley, and our now-canceled plans as we all sit down together. Dad pours three more cups of coffee into bulky mugs. It's all so undeniably relaxing, even at this hour.

It isn't long before light begins to peek through the small kitchen window, interrupting our conversation.

"Well, ol' Leon is expecting me in a few minutes, so I think we better mosey on down to the back," Ben says, looking over at his mother.

"And I guess I might as well go bury my head back under the covers," I remark, starting to rise from my chair.

"Oh no, that would be a shame! You look so nice," Cora responds. "Why don't I just take you to church with me? I'm sure Ben can get along just fine without me."

"Well… are you sure? I don't want to put anybody out," I ask earnestly, looking to my dad for approval.

"That would be great, Cora. She really needs some time out of the house," Dad says while grabbing his car keys from a small hook on the wall. "Why don't you take my car? Ben will be needing the truck this morning."

Within a few short minutes Cora and I are en route to her church. And though I'm still a little disappointed I won't be seeing Mrs. Paisley today, Ben's mother has such a kind and nurturing presence about her, which is so comforting to be around.

"I'm happy we are getting a chance to spend some time together, honey. Ben just thinks so much of you. He is always telling me how mature you are for your age," Cora remarks.

"Well, I like him a lot too. He's been so helpful to Dad and I both," I respond, smiling. It's sweet the way she doesn't try to conceal how proud she is of him.

Cora nods, keeping her eyes on the road ahead.

"Do you… mind if I ask you something, Ms. Cora?"

"Anything."

"What does Ben think about the… situation… *with Leon, I mean*. How does he feel about him being fired from Langley?" I ask tentatively.

Cora remains quiet for several seconds before clearing her throat. "Well… Ben and I both know that it's… complicated. No one ever wants to see a man lose his livelihood. *But* we certainly understand that from your father's perspective, he can't have someone working for him that he doesn't feel like he can trust. It's the hardest thing to earn and the easiest thing to lose," she says, looking a little less cheerful than usual. "We just hope the best for him… and for Langley as well."

"I hope we can take care of the estate like Cece and Carl would have wanted. The home meant so much to them," I say, feeling a bit low at the thought of my aunt.

"Well, that's all that matters, dear—the *want to*. If you and your dad have the desire to uphold the integrity of Langley, then I know that you will," she says, sounding chipper once again.

***

Following the early church service, Cora took me to a potluck lunch that was being held at the home of a friend of hers. It was mostly older ladies in attendance, as well as a few of their husbands. I thoroughly enjoyed interacting with them all, as her friends were so welcoming. They seemed genuinely interested in getting to know me.

I haven't had a lot of opportunities lately to interact with many people. So as an extravert, it was very much needed. And it seemed as though Cora really enjoyed having me there as well. She took every opportunity she could to brag on me in front of her friends.

Upon our arrival back at Langley, I notice that Ben's trailer is parked in front of the house, *empty*. Though I can tell that it had, in fact, made its way to Leon's cottage and then back onto the main road–as evidenced by tire marks left in the snow. It's hard to tell in the daylight, but there doesn't appear to be any lights on in Leon's former home.

Cora and I make it up the front porch steps of the estate before we are greeted by Ben, who offers us each a hand as we carefully avoid patches of ice. My father soon emerges at the front door as well, anxious to hear about my day.

The four of us congregate in the formal living room. I remove my new coat from Fireflies before taking a seat in front of the fireplace.

"How was church, Mom?" Ben asks, smiling.

"It was wonderful. And I had a popular guest with me to boot," Cora responds.

I try to remain patient while my father has Cora fill him in on our time spent together, though I'm dying to ask Ben how the move went this morning. Has Leon cooled down at all? Where did Ben help him move his stuff to? Does Leon want our heads served up on a platter!?

"Well, I'm so glad this all worked out—thanks to you, Cora," my father says, smiling over at her.

"I'd love to do it again sometime if that's alright with you," I add.

"*Anytime*," Cora responds, seemingly excited at the prospect.

"So, *Ben...*" I begin cautiously, trying to avoid coming across as overeager. "How did it go helping Leon this morning?"

"Oh, not too bad," Ben says, suddenly looking a bit downtrodden. Though he may just be tired. "He has a storage unit on the other side of town. I remember he got it after his folks died and left him some things. He mainly needed somewhere to keep all the furniture that wouldn't fit in his cottage. That's where we stopped first after we got everything loaded up," he adds.

"You moved all his things to a storage unit?" Cora asks, concerned.

"Everything but a suitcase. He had me drop him off at the hotel after that," Ben replies.

"Wait, he has a truck, doesn't he?" Cora asks, sounding increasingly worried.

"He does, but it's in the shop. He hardly ever has a need to drive it, and it's pretty dated," Ben responds. "I told him to call me if he needs a ride to the mechanic shop when it's ready... or in the meantime."

Dad is listening and nodding politely during our conversation, but remains quiet. I know he feels responsible—*though he has no reason to*. Letting Leon go was the only option.

"That was nice of you, Ben," I say, hoping to lift his spirits.

No matter what Leon has said or done, my aunt obviously saw *something* good in him to have kept him on for all these years. I just hope we aren't letting her down.

We are all a bit startled as the sound of our doorbell ringing disrupts the conversation.

"Who could that be on a Sunday afternoon?" my father asks, heading for the front door.

As I enter the foyer, I can see that Dad is greeting two uniformed police officers. I remember their faces from the other morning. They had both responded to the call after our animals were killed.

"How you doing, Ben?" one of the officers asks as my father shuts the door behind them.

"Not too bad, Hank. Do you have news for us?" Ben responds hopefully.

"We got the toxicology report back," Hank says, glancing over at his partner before continuing. "It seems as though your animals were poisoned... and it was almost certainly intentional. The amount of antifreeze in their systems could have easily taken out a rhino."

The news seems to hit us all like a ton of bricks. I feel a bit nauseated as I listen to my father and Ben asking the officers follow-up questions. Cora moves over to me and places her hand gently on my shoulder.

I try to stop myself from crying as I notice pressure building just below my eyes, intensifying with every passing moment. My aunt loved Langley's animals—and the fact that we couldn't keep them safe for her feels almost unbearable.

I wish Thomas was here to get this news alongside me. He sent me a text just as Cora and I were sitting down for church this morning, so I let him know that I would get in touch once we had returned home.

Though I think we all knew that poisoning was a likely scenario, the confirmation is still difficult to accept. It's hard to believe that anyone could be so cruel. So sinister. And for what reason? What could they have hoped to gain, except perhaps some sort of revenge on the estate—but for what?

"We didn't have a chance to speak with your groundskeeper the other morning—*Leon?*" the second officer says while reading from his notepad. "Is he around by chance? Maybe he has some ideas? Or knows someone we might want to look into?"

His questions are met with a pregnant pause.

"Leon is no longer employed here, unfortunately," Dad finally answers.

The officer exchanges a quick glance with his partner before scribbling something down.

"Well, nonetheless we'd like to speak with him," Officer Hank responds. "Perhaps you could provide us with a phone number or address."

Ben and my father give them the requested information, while I say my goodbyes to Cora. All I want is to retreat to my room and change into something more comfortable than panty hose, heels, and a fitted dress.

I'm welcomed by the sweet aroma of vanilla as I make it to my room. The essential oil diffuser housed on my dresser has been running all day, and provides a calming environment in which to wind down. Though I made my bed this morning, I can tell that the throw blanket at the end has been re-folded, and the fancy throw pillows are arranged in a more aesthetically-pleasing way. One of the part-time housekeepers must have been here today.

I leave my shoes and hose in a pile on the floor before stretching out at the foot of my bed. After burying my face in the perfectly-folded throw blanket, I turn to locate my cell phone.

Despite the fact that I'm feeling undeniably low, I really should text Thomas and fill him in on the latest news.

***

The next day, Thomas joined me at Langley right after school. We had a lot to talk about, none of which included a mention of our kiss two days prior. Nonetheless, there was a definite shift in our relationship—an unspoken secret between the two of us.

Thomas, of course, had no doubt as to the culprit who poisoned the innocent animals of my aunt's estate.

"But, Leon's loyalty to Cece runs much deeper than we ever knew. He was... in love with her," I say, making no attempt to hide my disgust at the mere thought. "Would he really hurt *her* animals?"

Thomas has been pacing back and forth around the living room for the past ten minutes.

"You never know what a psycho like that may be thinking, Greer. He's... *deranged.* I have half a mind to go have a chat with him myself. He can't just disappear scot-free," Thomas replies.

"You're not doing *that*," I respond, though I appreciate how much he cares. "This is bigger than either one of us. *And*, I know for a fact that the police will be contacting him, if they haven't already."

He nods his head, though still clearly discouraged. "Your aunt and uncle took great care of this place... but I sure wish they would have installed security cameras. I just... feel like the police might have a hard time *proving* he did it, even when it's this obvious."

The kitchen door leading out to the yard can be heard slamming shut in dramatic fashion. It really has a mind of its own. Ben soon appears in the living room, carrying with him a plastic storage bin.

"How's it going you two? Have you recovered from yesterday, Greer?" Ben asks.

"Not hardly," I respond (being perfectly honest).

Ben nods sympathetically. "Well, Thomas, do you think your mother wants these decorations in here?" he asks.

"Sorry, no idea. What are they?" Thomas inquires.

"Valentine's Day in this bin. Then I have two more to bring in with Easter decorations," he says, looking through the clear plastic. "She wanted me to go ahead and get what she'll need for the next few months down from the attic."

"You all sure are festive around here," I quip.

"Well, you know how your aunt loved the holidays. Putting up those Christmas lights was a two-day project for me and Leon," he responds, but quickly looks down at his feet as though unsure of whether or not he should mention him.

"I know you must miss having Leon here. It's not fair for you to have to take on the extra work," I tell him. "I can talk to my dad about looking for someone to replace him, sooner rather than later."

"No, it's no rush," Ben replies. "I had already taken over most of the heavy lifting anyway. Though he *was* really good at keeping us on track. I never had to think about how to space chores throughout the week, for instance. But I don't mind taking over all of that."

"Didn't he used to take care of all the vehicles? Oil changes and that sort of thing," Thomas asks.

"*He did.* Like I said–he was really good at keeping a schedule. He always knew when Mrs. Cecilia's car was due for any maintenance," Ben responds. "I was honestly surprised he needed to put his own truck in the shop last week. But I suppose good upkeep can only take you so far, until the ravages of time catch up."

"That's true," Thomas adds as he takes a seat. "Do you know what was wrong with it?"

"*I don't…* and Leon didn't either, which is why he finally conceded to taking it in. Though, I believe he started having trouble with it right after Christmas Day. So, you can imagine why it's taken him this long to address it," Ben says.

"Oh… *the accident,*" Thomas replies.

"Yes… he was in a really bad place. I've never seen a man more broken."

"But, why would he have been driving on Christmas Day–just after she died?" I ask curiously.

"Well, he… drove to the crash site actually–even though the roads were unfit," Ben replies.

"But *why* would he do that?" Thomas asks, seeming a tad flustered.

"I think he needed to see it with his own eyes– where she passed away," Ben replies. "Anyway, his truck ended up sliding off the road into a ditch. He called me to come pull it out. He thinks something must have happened that day to cause the problems he's been having with it. Says it's not steering right. But personally, I think it's just old."

As Ben heads back to the attic to fetch the remaining decor for Anne-Marie, I can't help but to question why Leon chose to drive to the crash site if he was so distraught. It seems a bit morbid to me, whether or not he had romantic feelings for her. It seems–*obsessive,* even.

"Speaking of my mom, I should have asked Ben where she's hiding," Thomas says as he stretches out on the living room couch and rubs his face.

"She's in the office with my dad, again," I respond coolly.

Anne-Marie seems so keen on helping him get the estate's business affairs in order, a fact of which I've been trying in vain to ignore. She's Thomas's mother, a loyal employee, and she's always treated me well. I know Dad needed help clearing up the floor and desk space in Uncle Carl's office (which is understandable). But now it seems as though they're getting a bit more technical, such as filing away documents and taking phone calls (on speakerphone) with Cece's accountant. I don't want to be suspicious of her, but after the hell that Leon has put us through it's hard not to examine the motives of everyone around us.

I doubt that Thomas would share in my paranoia regarding his mother. And I would never want to hurt either one of them with unfounded accusations. But, at the very least, I feel a responsibility to my dad, and to Langley, to be on the lookout for potential snakes in the grass. *Just like Leon.*

CHAPTER ELEVEN

"How could this have happened again!?" Ben yells, burying his face into his cupped hands and pacing quickly around the backyard.

"Have you called the police yet?" my father asks frantically as he pulls his cell phone from his jacket pocket.

"Don't worry about it, Owen. I'll take care of it," Ben replies, taking the phone and walking towards the side of the house.

"How!? And... WHY!?" Anne-Marie screams loudly, tears beginning to roll down her face.

She and Dad are both clearly in shock. I guess maybe I am too. I stand motionless just behind the two of them. *Nothing I could say or do will make this better for anyone.* So, I simply look on—faced with yet another piece of evidence that there is indeed *someone* out to get us.

Gertie lies dead a few feet in front of our feet. And, yet again, there are no signs of trauma. This time, it was Ben who made the discovery. He called out to the rest of us from the kitchen doorway in a panic.

I know I should probably stay, but all I want is to retreat back upstairs and into my comfortable bedding. I may even try to convince myself that it was all just a bad dream. Either way, more sleep is what I crave the most. I'll let Dad and Ben handle it.

I don't know that I've ever felt as helpless as I do right now. These things keep happening, and there's simply nothing I can do to change any of it. I immediately text Thomas once I'm upstairs. He's lucky he's at school right now and not the estate.

I can sense his frustration and sadness even through text messaging. So after giving him the facts, I drop the subject so that he can focus on schoolwork. It's not as though he can help either.

***

About twenty minutes have passed since I made it back into the warm embrace of my upstairs bedroom. The siren of a police car can be heard echoing throughout the grounds. Dad, Anne-Marie, and Ben are still talking in the backyard.

I wonder if the police have spoken with Leon. How long will he stay at the hotel? Is he answering his cell phone?

The last time this happened, Leon was living and working at Langley. It would have been all too easy for him to have poisoned the animals' food or water. But with Gertie–did he drive back here late at night? Does he even have access to a vehicle right now?

Eventually I drift off to sleep, leaving behind a reality I would love to escape for as long as possible. Though it may not be the healthiest trauma response, I suppose there are worse ways to escape than sleep.

***

"What did the police have to say?" I ask reluctantly.

I slept for nearly two hours before waking to a quiet house. The stairs leading to the ground floor felt as cold as ever against my bare feet. I find my father sitting at his desk working, the despair apparent in his expression.

"They're looking into it, of course," he says, glancing up from the paperwork scattered in front of him. "They'll confirm whether or not she was killed by the same poison as the others."

"I just... I don't get it. Any of it. Who could do this?" I ask, pleading for some sort of explanation.

"Only a very sick person could have done this, hun," he responds solemnly. "Your aunt loved old Gertie... and the fact that I couldn't even keep her (or any of the other animals) safe... *it kills me*."

"This isn't your fault, Dad," I say, getting emotional.

"I just think... no, I *know* that your grandpa would have done a better job. It was always supposed to be him," he says, shaking his head.

"No one could have prevented this—not even Grandpa. Not when there's someone out there with some sort of demented resolve to make our lives miserable," I protest.

"Well, we'll figure it all out. The only thing I want you focused on is schoolwork," he says, managing a smile.

I wonder how he'd feel if he knew about Thomas. We've never really talked about dating, though he may have been hoping Mrs. Paisley would cover the topic.

"Where's Anne-Marie?"

"The grocery store. She was pretty upset earlier. So I think she needed to get out and clear her head," he responds. "But she should be back any minute."

"She's been... spending a lot of time helping you lately," I say, trying to dig for information without being too obvious.

"Yeah, she's been great. She's really got a knack for taking a mess and making some sense out of it."

"That's true. One day she organized my makeup that was scattered all around my bathroom. Now it looks like a MAC counter," I say with a grin.

He lets out a short chuckle before turning to face me. "So, have you liked living here? I mean, if you try to put aside what's been going on. I mean... are you starting to feel like its home?" Dad asks.

There's so much hope in his voice–more than I've heard in a long time. But the truth is, I can't just put it all aside. I can't compartmentalize the deaths of Grandpa Frank, Cece... our animals. Their passing taints every day spent at Langley. And while most would love to live in a home of such beauty and grandeur, the way in which we came to live here makes it virtually impossible to appreciate.

As much as I want to express to him the difficulty I've had settling in, I can't be selfish by adding to his list of burdens.

"Oh, sure. I mean, you know I've always loved this house. And my room makes me feel like I'm 'Eloise' living at The Plaza Hotel," I say smiling. "And–you're here–which is one thing Langley has going for it that our old house never did."

"I know I haven't been present as much as I should have because of work. And, your grandpa did such a great job taking care of you. The two of you were thick as thieves–and you always seemed so happy and well-adjusted," Dad replies.

"Don't worry–*I was*. I am. But it's nice having you around all the time now," I add.

I'm relieved my response seems to have perked him up a bit. And I'm hoping that in time, Langley will, indeed, feel like home. Though as of now, I don't think the house and I have been given a fair chance to bond, given the never-ending tragedies that surround it.

It isn't long before Anne-Marie can be heard unloading grocery bags in the kitchen. As Dad and I join her, I can tell she's feeling better than she was earlier in the day.

"How do you like chicken tetrazzini, Greer?" she asks warmly.

"I've only ever had it at the country club… but I'm a fan," I reply, mustering a smile.

"As I'm sure you've gathered, we aren't picky eaters," my father adds while putting away pantry items.

"We've never eaten better than we have since moving here."

Anne-Marie smiles, her cheeks turning a touch pink.

"Will you and Thomas be staying for dinner?" Dad asks.

"Well, I hadn't really thought about it just yet. But… I don't see why not," she responds happily.

Although I'm keen on the idea of spending some time with Thomas this evening, it seems as though the relationship between my father and Anne-Marie is… evolving. They're getting closer, and I've found myself experiencing a wide range of emotions in response.

I really want to trust her. Though with my father's new position at the estate, it's difficult not to question her interest in him. Yet I find myself enjoying the undeniable warmth she brings to our lives. It's as though she's Langley's surrogate 'lady of the house.' She not only keeps the home clean and running, but also puts a lot of thought and care into making it feel less like a museum and more like a family home.

Thomas joined me at the house after school. He was anxious to hear all the details surrounding Gertie's death, though I really didn't have anything to share apart from what I let him know through text that morning.

"Have the police been in touch with Leon?" he asks as he hoists himself up onto the trampoline.

Despite the cold, we're both tired of spending all our time indoors. He's bundled up in his school jacket, wearing a red hoodie underneath. His thick hair sweeps up and over the hood, which is pulled tightly around his face. His cheeks are pink, and his lips shiver slightly as he speaks.

When he suggested sitting on the trampoline I layered two long-sleeved t-shirts under a plain white hoodie, paired with black jeans. I had already spent an embarrassing amount of time on my hair and makeup before his arrival. After fighting with my long locks for over half an hour, I finally pulled it all away from my face into two french braids.

"I don't know… I didn't stick around to talk to them. I just went back to bed," I tell him, burrowing my hands into my pockets. He and I are sitting relatively close together, though not touching.

He still hasn't acknowledged our kiss, and at this point the thought of him coming right out and mentioning it sounds humiliating. Though of course, pretending it never happened at all would certainly be the least desirable scenario.

"I hope he hasn't skipped town," he says, sounding frustrated.

"I'm sure the police are on top of it. I mean… crime isn't exactly running rampant in this town, is it?" I ask.

"No," he replies with a grin. "Apart from traffic stops and old folks calling them because kids are out rolling houses, this should be priority number one."

I can hardly feel my hands as I brush a strand of hair away from my face. The wind has picked up. I squint as my eyes begin to water and the cold slaps my face. The netting surrounding the trampoline does absolutely nothing to slow its determination to usher us back inside the house.

"Let's go," Thomas says, hurriedly making his way to the exit.

Once his feet hit the ground below he offers me his hand, and I've suddenly become very aware of the fact that there is no graceful way to exit a trampoline. All I can do is hope that I don't look as awkward as I feel.

The sky has spent the past half hour turning a subtle shade of gray. The sun is hidden, yet I can find not a single distinguishable cloud. It's just an even layer of gray hanging in the sky, like oil floating on water. Though dreary, it's somehow calming as the wind below makes such a fuss, moving about in every direction.

I take a moment to get one final look at the perfectly still gray sky as Thomas helps me down. It takes me a second to realize that he hasn't moved. He's standing in front of me, never having let go of my hand. The wind whips past us as though offended we haven't yet begun sprinting towards the warm house.

Though still numb, a certain warmth overtakes my body as he looks at me. I'd been waiting for some sort of acknowledgment of what occurred between us, and here it is. My back is still resting on the trampoline as he gently lifts my hand and kisses my palm before placing it on his own cheek.

His hood still surrounds his face, covering his ears. I can do nothing else but stare back at him, despite the freezing wind and darkening sky above us. It feels like we'll never make it back inside, yet neither one of us cares. It's like being in a trance in which I'm unable, or perhaps just unwilling, to acknowledge that anything else exists apart from the two of us.

Despite our shared determination to remain engulfed in this current state of being, mother nature has seemingly had enough. A single raindrop hits my face like an unexpected knock at the front door, and we are both jolted back to reality.

Thomas squeezes my hand tightly as he turns toward the house and we both begin running. The sky has opened up like a broken levee. He opens the side door and ushers me inside before pulling it tightly closed behind us.

The rain is picking up speed by the second as we take a moment to catch our breath. We're both shivering as we kick off our drenched socks and shoes. Several seconds pass before I'm even aware that we have an audience. My father and Anne-Marie are both seated in the kitchen, looking particularly amused by our current state. A pot of coffee sits between them, radiating heat and filling the room with its scent.

Did they see us on the trampoline? I have a feeling that Thomas is similarly concerned, as he gives me a knowing glance.

"I didn't know you two were out there! *Are you crazy?*" Anne-Marie asks jokingly.

A look of relief flashes across his face. "We just needed some fresh air, Mom. But then we got a little more than we bargained for."

"I guess *so*," my dad chimes in. "Greer, why don't you head on up to your room and get changed out of those wet clothes."

***

When I return to the kitchen, I find Thomas drinking a cup of coffee, my father sitting beside him—laser focused on the crossword puzzle he's working on. Thomas is now wearing a dry t-shirt and a pair of basketball shorts.

"Where's your mom?" I ask.

"Getting my clothes started in the dryer," he says, looking up from his coffee mug. "Thankfully, I had these shorts in my bag... otherwise I would have had to borrow something from Mr. Owen's closet."

We both laugh as my father fails to respond, never even glancing away from his small crossword book. A shiver suddenly overtakes my body, starting at the soles of my feet. Dry clothes or not, *I'm still freezing*. I had changed into a loungewear set—a pair of loose-fitting pants and matching top which ties at the bottom—but it doesn't seem to be enough.

"Hey, Dad—do I still have a few boxes left in the garage?" I ask, breaking his concentration.

"I'm not sure... *maybe*. Why do you ask?" he responds.

"I can't find my slippers... and I hate just wearing socks to go up and down the stairs. I've nearly died three times," I say in jest.

"Yeah, they are a bit slick I suppose. But you're welcome to go look," he says. "I'm still bringing one or two of my boxes inside every few days to unpack. Thomas—will you help her look?"

"Sure thing, Mr. Owen," Thomas replies before rinsing out his coffee mug in the sink.

Langley's 'garage' feels less like a place in which to park one's vehicle and more like a commercial warehouse. No less than eight vehicles could be parked in the space if needed. There are a large number of organized storage bins lined up on shelving attached to the walls. Each bin is adorned with a printed label describing its contents.

Pushed against one corner of the garage are cardboard boxes of various sizes, which Ben had helped unload from our rented moving truck. Though due to the fact that Langley is more than adequately stocked with furnishings, pots and pans, and other home essentials, the vast majority of these items have remained in their cardboard dwellings—at least those we didn't have the time or energy to sell.

I felt certain I had identified all of the boxes containing my own personal items the day we arrived. Yet my house slippers, along with a few pairs of dress shoes, have still failed to turn up.

"So, what should I be on the lookout for?" Thomas asks, crouching down to read the words etched in Sharpie marker on the sides of the boxes.

"It should say something along the lines of '*Greer's closet; Greer's shoes*' …but of course they could also be packed in a random box along with our throw pillows and coffee maker," I quip.

"Well, let's hope that's not the case," Thomas replies.

"At least my dad has been working on unpacking all of his things. The last time I was in here there were *a lot* more boxes."

I had stored my painting of the small yellow house I was working on in the garage. It wasn't quite finished yet, and I didn't want to bring a wet painting inside the house. There is a narrow closet within the garage which I had discovered was completely barren apart from several large paint cans resting on a shelf. The cans were labeled, noting which room of the home the paint color belonged to. The largest was a white bucket labeled, '*Foyer; Living Rooms.*' I determined it would be the ideal place to store my easel and paints where they would be out of the way.

"This one says '*Greer/ Miscellaneous,*'" Thomas exclaims, just as I was about ready to give up the search.

"Yes! That must be it," I reply, downright giddy at the thought of recovering my lost slippers.

Upon opening the cardboard box, I immediately spot several pairs of dress shoes, as well as a pair of cream-colored flats. An old notebook of mine is pressed up against one side of the box, and a few crayons and markers glide along the bottom with every movement. *Dad must have packed this one.*

Though it takes a minute of digging, I finally find my slippers buried at the bottom of the moving box. They're a bit misshapen due to all the weight placed on top of them, but I'm sure they'll recover quickly.

"Success?" Thomas asks hopefully.

"Yes! This is them. And I'm happy to have found the rest of it too."

Thomas grabs the large box from the floor, placing it under his arm.

"Well, let's get this on up to your room. The garage is freezing!" he exclaims before walking quickly toward the door.

"I just need to grab my easel real quick. I left a painting to dry in here," I reply.

Opening the door to the small closet off to one side of the massive garage, I stand frozen as I stare into the tiny space. The shelving which once supported at least a dozen large paint cans is now on the floor. Most of the paint is pooled and splattered amongst the broken shelves.

I can only locate bits and pieces of my dismembered easel. In fact, the only thing *not* amongst the debris is my painting itself. It is hanging prominently in the middle of the wall, where the shelves used to be. Two words written in black paint now cover the majority of the canvas. The quaint yellow house is barely visible underneath.

"Greer? What are you..." Thomas says before stopping dead in his tracks just behind me. "What in the hell!?"

He drops my box filled with shoes to the ground before moving further into the closet than I've been able to. It's almost as if he wants to protect me from the scene before us, although it's already too late.

"'*You're next!*' What is *that* supposed to mean?" Thomas asks rhetorically.

That is the phrase which now covers the canvas– '*You're Next!*'

The perpetrator seems to have haphazardly scribbled the words using one of my own paintbrushes and a small tube of black oil paint, which are currently amongst the debris.

"Could you go get my dad?" I ask, my eyes undoubtedly gleaming with unshed tears.

As Thomas disappears into the house, all I can think of is how much I want to go home. All of this was thrust upon me without warning, and now I'm being terrorized by an unknown enemy who is clearly out for blood.

It doesn't take long before my father and Anne-Marie make it to the garage. Anne-Marie looks as though she's on the brink of a panic attack. She takes a seat against the wall as her breathing grows heavier. Thomas rushes over to comfort her as she collapses.

Dad hasn't said a word as he surveys the damage. His face has turned a worrisome shade of ghostly-white.

"Was this yours, Greer?" he finally asks.

"Yes… I put it in here to dry," I tell him.

Dad pulls his cell phone from his pocket as though it's a bomb requiring immediate diffusion. It seems he is moving rapidly from shock to anger as he calls the police station.

Thomas leaves to fetch Ben, as Anne-Marie ushers me back inside the house. I grab my slippers from the floor and gladly make my way to the living room fireplace. My feet are almost entirely without feeling, as I'd spent much longer barefoot in the garage than I had anticipated.

I plop myself down on the floor, directly in front of the fire. As I slide my newly-recovered slippers onto my feet, I think back on my evening spent chasing Leon barefoot out into the cold—or chasing no one out into the cold. I still have a hard time believing that a man his age could have disappeared so quickly. Maybe my mind really was playing tricks on me. I was tired... and probably a little paranoid after the electricity went out.

The idea that he's been sneaking back onto the property undetected in order to poison the animals, break into the garage, and vandalize my painting seems similarly unlikely. Everyone who works at Langley knows that Leon is no longer allowed on the grounds. He would have been seen. Could someone be helping him? Or does Leon have nothing to do with any of this at all, and is merely guilty of being a grumpy, disenfranchised old man?

CHAPTER TWELVE

The storm outside has picked up a lot over the last several hours. Thomas and I have been texting back and forth since he and his mother left for the day. *I appreciate the way texting takes the pressure off of a conversation.*

It's just so informal. Texting is like the t-shirt and jeans form of communication. You can reply to a text within five minutes or five hours—and in most cases both are perfectly acceptable. Though, I do wish I could speak to Thomas over the phone a bit more. However, neither my father or Anne-Marie has been made aware of the evolving relationship between Thomas and myself—and spending hours on the phone together would likely be a dead giveaway.

Dad rarely asks who I'm texting with—and when he does, I usually just name one of my girlfriends from the country club. Though, I do throw Thomas in there from time to time—just so I feel like less of a liar. I'm just not ready to share my feelings towards him yet (with anyone), especially since I've not quite come to terms with them myself.

My eyelids have grown heavy over the past half hour. Though the weather outside is intense, it's undeniably soothing as I disappear into my fancy covers and pillows. All of the lights are off in my bedroom apart from a lamp resting on my bedside table.

Just as I'm about to try and wrap up my conversation with Thomas, the lamp begins to flicker on and off. I peep my head out from under the covers, hoping there's no one standing next to my bed ready to snatch me up. Looks like the electricity is going out again.

The police have been patrolling our street since yesterday, after we called them (yet again) about the vandalization of my painting—and of the garage. I suppose they deemed it necessary following the not-so-thinly-veiled threat of '*You're next*' graffitied on the wall.

It does make me feel better knowing that there are officers keeping watch over the estate while the house sleeps. We've proven time and time again to be vulnerable. Although the main house was thoroughly searched, police were unable to find any clues as to *who* may have broken in, nor *how* they did it. Apart from a trashed garage closet, wasted paint, and a now-useless painting, nothing else was amiss.

Once photos were taken of the scene, the chief gave Anne-Marie the go-ahead to clean things up in the garage, which seemed to perk her up a bit. Personally, I would not want to tackle that mess—but I think cleaning helps to relieve her anxiety.

The storm seems to have peaked as I venture out of my bedroom—slippers keeping my feet warm against the hardwood. I can't find a single source of light on the second floor. I am able to see where I'm going solely by the light streaming gently through the windows of the guest rooms.

It's already past midnight, so I'm surprised to spot a bright light off in the distance. The property is typically pitch black at night. The closest home to Langley is the estate across the street, which is on the complete opposite side of where the light is coming from. I walk slowly towards the room which boasts the clearest view of the backyard, specifically the location of Leon's cottage.

I rub my eyes as I reach the window, hoping I'll wake up in my own bed. Hoping I'm dreaming. But nothing happens, because it's all too real.

Every window of the small home in the backyard is lit up like a firecracker, as though its previous tenant had never left. I stand at the glass for several minutes before the lights of the cottage begin to flicker on and off. My throat suddenly closes up, and my chest feels inexplicably weighted down. Who is in there!? Did Leon come back?

The names and phone numbers of the two officers patrolling our home for the night are scribbled on a piece of paper and stuck to the refrigerator downstairs. The senior officer instructed us to call if we had any issues arise.

Although my first instinct is to call them, I consider the fact that whoever has been terrorizing the estate is clearly very skilled at making a quick exit. If the officers were to drive to the cabin, even without lights on, I have no doubt that the squatter would quickly spot them. He will have disappeared into the night before the police even made it to the front door.

I need to catch him there, even if just to take a few pictures through the window before calling the officers. I practically sprint back to my room to grab my phone from the bed. In a way, it feels as though the house itself is (finally) on my side–pushing me forward with every step as I hastily pull an oversized sweatshirt over my head and slide on tennis shoes, wasting no time with socks.

I reach the first floor, trying my best to stay quiet. Even if the house *is* on my side, my tennis shoes are clearly trying to give me away as they pound against the floor. *I can't wake up Dad.* He would never allow me out of the house if he knew.

His bedroom door is closed, and all is silent as I take a brief moment to stand perfectly still in the hallway. I'm relieved there isn't even a hint of movement apart from my own labored breathing. I'm certain that adrenaline has, once again, overtaken my body. Despite my inability to fully catch my breath, I feel as though I could run a marathon.

I walk only on the balls of my feet until I reach the kitchen door. Taking a second to tighten the drawstring around my face, I push back flyaway hair into the hood. I then place my phone into the middle pocket of my sweatshirt before taking one final deep breath.

The elements waiting for me on the other side of the door are even worse than I'd expected. The wintry mix of rain and snow freezes against my skin. The cold is nearly unbearable–and unrelenting. The wind pushes the precipitation against my body in seemingly every direction. As I run, my shoes grow increasingly soaked by the second. I really should have taken the time to find rubber boots.

I can barely see where I'm going–guided only by the light of Leon's cottage. The freezing rain propels me forward as I manage to pick up speed. My feet seem to have numbed to the point of having little to no feeling.

The light inside the cottage is no longer flickering. I can barely look up as I make it within a few yards from the front door. I've never seen it so bright.

I slow to a jog as I crouch down for fear of being spotted. I set my sights on the window closest to me, to the left of the doorstep. I drop to my hands and knees as I make it to within a few feet.

The ground seems to be frozen solid, apart from the mixture of mud and snow that now covers my all-too-thin pajama pants and thick hoodie. I'm not entirely sure whether or not I'm still wearing shoes at this point, as I feel absolutely nothing below my kneecaps.

I push the top part of my body up slowly from the ground off of my stomach. As my eyes finally meet the bottom of the window, I'm half expecting Leon, or perhaps an accomplice, to be there waiting for me on the other side of the glass.

There is very little furniture left in the cabin. An old leather couch rests in the very center of the living area. A round, wooden table sits just off to the side of the kitchenette. Though it does not include a single dining chair, the table is filled with empty chip bags, candy wrappers, bottles, and various papers.

The walls of both the living and kitchen areas are littered with paperwork and photographs. There are several blankets strewn along the couch, yet it's hard to imagine the space being a livable environment for anyone walking on two legs. It's–*trashed*–completely trashed.

Ben would have told us if Leon had left it like this. Did he come back? Has he been staying here? And if not him, who HAS been staying here?

Though the lights are on, I've yet to detect any movement inside. After a minute or so of no activity, I walk slowly along the side of the house. I've officially lost all feeling in my legs as I make it to the only window at the back of the cottage.

I peer into the lone bedroom of the home just as carefully as I did at the front window. Apart from a few papers resting on the floor, it is completely empty. No furniture. *Nothing.* I can also see clear into the small en suite bathroom, which appears to be just as vacant as the bedroom.

There is nothing reflected in the plain mirror hanging just above the bathroom sink apart from beige, empty wall space. Even so, I keep my eyes fixated on the mirror for quite some time before I'm satisfied that Freddy Krueger won't suddenly appear.

There is no one inside—*at least for now.* Although I feel safe enough to stand up straight before venturing back towards the front, my heart is still pounding as I peer out into the darkness. I refuse to leave empty-handed when I'm so close to finding some answers. So, I hold my breath and slowly turn the front door knob. *It's unlocked.*

The interior of the cabin offers much-needed respite from the storm raging outside. I'm shivering from head to toe as I walk towards the living room wall, which contains the highest volume of defacement. My eyes immediately lock in on a group of photographs which are printed on computer paper and adhered to the wall via push pins.

Three of the photographs are partly obscured by 'X' marks, written in what appears to be a red Sharpie marker. As I get closer to the wall, my veins run cold once I'm able to make out clearly the smiling faces beneath the Xs.

It's photographs of Uncle Carl, Cece, and Grandpa Frank that have been graffitied over with red marker.

I also see my own face looking back at me. It's a photo which could easily have been taken from social media. I'm posing alongside Grandpa Frank in the snapshot—though the version hanging on the wall in front of me has cropped out most of his face, leaving only me— posing in front of our Christmas tree last year.

Photos of my father, Anne-Marie, Thomas, Ben, *and Leon* are also hanging sporadically along the wall in no distinguishable order. There is what appears to be a hand drawn map of the estate hanging to the right of the printed photographs. Incoherent scribbles cover most of the remaining papers littering the wall.

A torn piece of blue cardstock pinned next to Cece's photo appears to have the word 'Gertie' written erratically along the entire length of the paper. Though I try to make sense out of another note pinned next to it, I give up after several seconds. It would take much longer than I'm comfortable with to decipher anything else.

I hurriedly pull my phone from my pocket. I had not realized how badly I've been shaking until trying to keep my arm and hand still long enough to photograph the wall. I'm freezing, and terrified that someone will walk through the front door behind me at any given moment. I check over my shoulder every few seconds while continuing to document the evidence, *quite literally*, written on the wall. If someone can make sense of the scribblings, it will almost certainly aid us in identifying the author.

I slip my phone back into my pocket, more than ready to get back to the main house. Though just as I'm about to leave, I realize I've tracked in snow and mud behind me. And because I'd much prefer that the perpetrator *not* be made aware that I'm on to him, I quickly grab a half-empty roll of paper towels from the pile of trash on the kitchen table and get to work covering my tracks.

I'm now mostly numb in all of my extremities. I hurriedly drop to my knees and begin wiping aggressively at the mess. After about a minute or so I toss the remaining paper towel roll back on the table and stuff the wet towels in my sweatshirt pocket.

It seems to take much longer to return home than it did to make it down to Leon's cabin. Though once I finally reach the kitchen, I quickly lock the side door behind me before stripping off my clothes and sneakers as though they had caught fire. I place my phone on the kitchen countertop before ridding my pullover of wet paper towels.

After making it to the laundry room, I toss my soiled clothing and shoes into the washing machine. I then search the room frantically for something–*anything*– to cover myself up with before sprinting to my bedroom– but with no luck. So I obscure my body as best I can with my arms and try not to look around as I climb the steps to the warm bedroom waiting for me on the second story.

Though I had originally planned on bundling myself up with half of my winter wardrobe, I instead head straight for the bathroom and run a warm bath before making it back to my bed to wait on the tub to fill. *I've never been more uncomfortable in my life.* And I feel as though my body may be in a state of shock as I curl myself into a ball underneath the covers.

I really need to get in touch with the policemen patrolling the house to inform them of the new development on the property. But both my phone and their numbers are still in the kitchen downstairs. Apart from the shivering, I can't move. I must have made it back to the house solely in an innate survival mode.

I try to focus on the sound of water filling my bathtub rather than my current physical state. After mustering the strength to emerge from under the covers after several minutes, I make it to the tub and lower myself slowly into the water. Yet I quickly realize that instead of the soothing effect I'd been hoping for, I feel nothing but agonizing pain as my body is fully engulfed.

The pain prohibits me from immediately evacuating the tub. I cling tightly to the side in an attempt to hoist myself out, but I am unable to muffle my screams as I do so. I may die here. There's no coming back from this. They'll find my body sometime tomorrow, and the curse of Langley Estates will be the stuff of legend.

I'm dizzy, and so confused. I can't understand why this is happening to me—*why I can't get up.* I should have just stayed in my bed and warmed up gradually. But I'd forgotten to bring my phone with me to call the officers patrolling the house, and I was desperate to feel well enough to get dressed and make it back downstairs.

As I look up at the ceiling it appears to be changing from beige to blue right before my eyes. I don't know what's happening, but it feels as though I'm losing my mind. I close my eyes tightly, hoping to wake in a different location entirely. Somewhere safe. Somewhere free of pain.

I lay my head on the side of the tub, trying to at least stay conscious for as long as possible. It's then that I hear the sound of thunder roaring like a herd of wild horses racing up the staircase. I can barely make out the figure currently standing in the doorway to my bathroom. The outline of their frame grows increasingly hazy until everything goes completely black, *all at once.*

THE BIOGRAPHER

Sadie has remained quiet. She seems just as confused by what she's heard as she is intrigued. I bet she wonders how I can speak about such events with little emotion behind it. Yet for me, the past is what it is. And I've had to relive my trauma too many times to count—whether it be due to a nightmare, or even a smell or song which triggers an unwelcome memory.

As I've been speaking for quite some time at this point, I take a pause in order to grab a half-empty water bottle from the side table next to me. Meanwhile, Sadie clears her throat a bit awkwardly before taking the opportunity to interject.

"My goodness. I didn't know what to expect from our interview today… but your story has surprised me," she says before taking a drink from her own water bottle.

"It's not something I really talk about anymore. I've honestly been a bit surprised by certain things myself… certain details I haven't thought about in so long. Things I must have pushed just below the surface."

Sadie nods her head before looking down at her notes. "How did you feel after your painting was destroyed?" she asks.

"I felt the way anyone would in that situation I guess," I respond. "*I was scared.* There was someone who seemed to want to hurt me in some way. And I had no idea *why.*"

"I can't imagine dealing with that type of stress… especially as a teenager," Sadie replies. "And the night you visited Leon's cabin—*how did you make it out of the bathtub?*"

CHAPTER THIRTEEN

The smell of bleach fills my nostrils as I open my eyes gradually, trying to get acclimated to the light. Not only am I not in my own bed, I'm also no longer at Langley.

My hospital room is painfully muted and still. While a noiseless environment is typically meant to be calming, I find it wholeheartedly terrifying at the present moment. Dad is curled up on the couch next to a large window, clutching a blanket which barely extends past his kneecaps. A small, flat screen television is mounted in a corner of the room—currently playing the morning news on mute.

I take the time to carefully move each of my limbs, one by one. My body seems to be functioning properly, albeit a bit sluggishly. I'm not in any significant discomfort, which is a stark contrast to my previous state of consciousness, just before the lights all went out. I had felt quite certain that the pain I experienced last night would never stop—at least not until my soul had transitioned from its occupancy of my fragile body. I was sure that the image of my bathroom ceiling, and at last the figure standing in the doorway, would be the final scenes ever to register in my mind. I've been such a fool—there's no way to get around it.

I'm covered in a white bedsheet from the neck down, followed by several layers of blankets, one of which seems to be heated. There's an IV inserted into my left hand. Despite having been awake for several minutes, I continue to feel as though disconnected from my body.

I move my wrist around, hoping to feel a twinge of pain, if only to assure myself that I am, in fact, still alive.

Though I hate to wake up Dad, I'm desperate for human interaction. I can't imagine how frightened he must have been. I can only assume that he was the figure in the doorway, responding to my screams.

"Dad?" I say, softly at first as my voice breaks. "*Dad?*" I repeat.

As soon as his eyes meet mine he hops up hurriedly from the couch, throwing him slightly off balance. He looks as though he hasn't slept for a week.

"Greer!? You're awake! Thank goodness," he says, placing his hand on my shoulder.

"How did I get here?" I ask, pleading for answers.

"I woke up to the sound of you screaming last night. When I made it to your room, I found you passed out in the bathtub," he responds. "I picked you up and called for an ambulance. Your body was turning colors. You were freezing. I thought I had lost you."

I look down at my lap, hating myself for causing him such pain and worry.

"I'm so sorry I put you through that, Dad."

It is then that I come to the realization that not only did he spend at least several hours wondering if he would be burying his only daughter—but he had been put in the position of lifting my body lifeless from a bathtub, just as he'd done for my mother the day she died. I feel like a monster, as this was entirely my doing.

"What happened last night, Greer?" Dad asks. "Anne-Marie found your wet clothes in the washing machine early this morning. Why did you go out in the snow?"

"I'm sorry, Dad... I was at Leon's cottage," I reply hesitantly. There's no use in lying. I need to own up to my inexcusably poor judgment. I owe him that at least.

"What? *Why!?*" he replies in disbelief.

"Because the lights were all on. I saw them flickering right after our own power started to go out."

"So you... went back there alone?"

"Yes. I thought I could catch them... *the person staying there,*" I continue.

"Staying there?" he asks, leaning in closer. It's almost as if he's unsure that he heard me correctly.

"Yes. Someone has been staying there. I don't know if it's Leon or someone else... but it is definitely the person responsible for killing the animals. And for destroying my painting."

"How do you know, Greer?" he asks.

I take a pause before responding. As surprised as I am at my own carelessness, I have a feeling that he will be even more disappointed in me than I am in myself.

"Because I went inside," I reply. "Our photos are pinned to the living room wall. There's a map of the estate. There are papers scattered everywhere–all with some kind of scribblings. I couldn't make out much of anything, but I took photos with my phone."

Dad places his head in his hands before looking back up at me. "That was very dangerous what you did. You should have come to me," he responds at last.

I nod my head in agreement, feeling ashamed. "My phone should still be on our kitchen counter. I left it there before taking off my wet clothes. I was just trying to get warm," I tell him, trying to explain myself in some way.

"The doctor said you were in the early stages of hypothermia, Greer. The bath water warmed you up way too quickly and your body went into shock."

I take a few moments for his words to settle in. I really am fortunate my stupidity didn't get me killed.

"Wow. If I had known how bad off I really was I never would have... *I'm sorry, Dad.*"

"There's plenty of time for us to talk about all that later. I'm just relieved that you're okay," he says flatly.

"Yes... thanks to you," I reply, managing a grin.

"I'm going to let the nurses know that you're awake," he says, rising from the tiny hospital couch.

"No, Dad! First you have to call the policemen patrolling the house... or the chief. Just... make sure they get someone out to Leon's cabin immediately. This guy may still be out there," I plead, praying my efforts won't be a total loss.

Dad concedes and makes the call as he's walking towards the door. "I still need to get someone in here to check on you," he says before disappearing into the hallway.

I just can't wrap my head around everything I saw last night. The state of the cottage. The photos. It all feels so unreal. I'm certain that losing consciousness soon after making it back to the main house has contributed to my current state of disconnection with the events of the evening.

Dad returns a few minutes later, his phone still glued to his ear.

"Okay, they're sending the two officers patrolling the house to go check out the cottage right now," he says, waiting in the doorway for a nurse.

A woman with dark hair and purple scrubs soon emerges. She takes my vital signs before proceeding to examine my limbs and torso.

"Don't worry about anything except feeling better," Dad says, taking his seat back on the couch. "Anne-Marie and Thomas have been so worried about you. They've called practically every half hour asking for updates. They wanted to come up here but I convinced them to hold things down at the house."

"That's nice," I respond awkwardly, unsure of what to say.

"Thomas didn't even make it to school. He's just been waiting it out with his mother. *In fact*, let me get a hold of Anne-Marie. I'll be back soon," he says, once again taking his leave.

Though still clearly in a heightened state of anxiety, I think staying on the phone is comforting for my father. He is keeping himself busy while also taking back some small piece of control in an otherwise chaotic situation.

The guilt I feel for being the cause of his current state will take considerable time to subside, I expect. All I can hope for now is that my misguided efforts won't be in total vain. If only the police are able to apprehend the suspect due to the knowledge that he has been residing in Langley's cottage (or even just move them one step closer to an arrest), we will all sleep better at night.

***

It's Friday morning before I'm able to return home to Langley. Anne-Marie and Thomas were able to visit me yesterday at the hospital, but otherwise I've been isolated without my phone. Though Anne-Marie searched, she was unable to find it. Not in the kitchen— not anywhere apparently.

Despite it being just days ago, the details of that evening seem to be evaporating from my memory at an alarming rate. I assume it has something to do with the fact that my poor body was exposed to such trauma. It seems to have disregarded what it considered to be insignificant information. I was in pure survival mode.

Even so, I feel certain I left my phone on the kitchen counter before peeling the freezing, wet clothes from my body in the laundry room. And the fact that it wasn't where I said it would be has left me questioning everything. Could the person staying in the cottage have stolen it from the house? Maybe they caught me snooping and waited until Dad and I left via ambulance that night. Luckily for them, all of my evidence and potential clues as to their identity were contained within that phone.

To make matters worse, Dad informed me that upon searching the cottage the police had turned up with absolutely nothing. No evidence of anyone staying there. No mess. No photos plastered across the wall. Nothing but the living room couch and kitchen table. The squatter would have had one night to clean it out before officers arrived the next morning.

If this person did, in fact, steal my phone (therefore knowing that I was aware of his living arrangements) it makes sense that he would have emptied his hideout in a hurry. Yet the only proof I have now of what I saw in Leon's former home is my word—*my* recollection of that night.

I've wondered if everyone thinks the entire scenario is a mere figment of my imagination. I overheard the doctor telling Dad that I could have experienced a hyper-realistic dream whilst in my unconscious state. And honestly, I've started to question myself as to whether or not everything occurred just as I recall. It wouldn't be the first time my mind has played tricks on me recently.

I felt certain I'd caught Leon red-handed snooping around my father's window in the dead of night, only to realize that there was no one to be found. And now there's a perfectly clean cabin, and no cell phone in sight to either confirm or dispute my sanity.

Upon my return to Langley, Dad presented me with a light blue gift box held together by an ivory ribbon.

I'd just made it to my bedroom and settled underneath the covers when Anne-Marie and Thomas joined us, followed by Ben. Contained within the gift box was a new cell phone; as well as a trendy, patterned phone case.

"I searched everywhere for your old phone, sweetie. I'm sorry I couldn't find it," Anne-Marie says as I look down at my brand-new home screen.

"That's okay. Thank you for trying. Guess I'll need to get all of your phone numbers again," I say in jest.

I can hardly wait until I'm able to speak with Thomas alone. *I'm sure he feels the same.* He was texting with me one minute, then just hours later his mother is informing him that I'm in intensive care. He is certainly owed an explanation, no matter how unsatisfying I expect it will prove to be.

The best I can hope for is that he doesn't think I'm crazy, even if I'm not so convinced myself. Does he believe my recollection of events? Does he believe that someone must have stolen the photographic evidence, and then proceeded to clean out the cottage before the police made it there the next morning?

I'm starting to think that despite its majestic appearance, Langley has pushed me so far beyond the limits of what I'd previously known to be a relatively safe existence, that I've been left with no boundaries in which to decipher reality from my own imagination. Has my interpretation of events over the past several weeks been skewed (thanks to a home which desires only to destroy each and every one of its occupants)?

My heart sinks as Dad ushers my visitors into the hallway in order to give me "time to rest." It has been absolute torture being forced to remain in bed the last couple of days. I want to figure all of this out. I need to prove to everyone, including myself, that I'm not delusional.

I manage to remain in bed with only my thoughts to keep me company for a mere half an hour before I make my way to my closet in search of something to change into. I feel certain that wearing clothing other than nightgowns and loungewear will aid in my goal of feeling a bit more human than I have in quite some time.

I lock eyes on one of my more casual dresses, hanging delicately near the back of the closet. I waste no time in throwing it on and heading straight for the bathroom in search of my makeup and flat iron. I can't let *him* win—even if I don't know who *he* is.

I nearly caught the person responsible for terrorizing the estate, and he slipped through my fingers. I resented the fact that I'd been forced to remain idle since that night, knowing it was due to my own carelessness. I can't fail Cece again. I can't allow this person to get the better of me—of all of us.

After taking some time to fix myself up, I grab my new phone and excitedly pass through my doorway in search of Thomas. I quickly find him in a nearby bedroom with his laptop and several books spread out on the bed.

"I'm sorry you've had to miss school because of me," I say as he looks up from his keyboard.

He quickly hops off the bed and greets me with a long embrace as I enter the room. It's even better than I'd imagined it—*our reunion*. I find myself thoroughly intoxicated by the smell of his cologne, along with the sound of his heart beating in his chest.

"Are you kidding?" he asks, smiling. "My mom called the school and they've allowed me to attend virtually the past few days," he says, taking a step back to look me in the eyes. "I... don't think I've ever been more worried in my life," he says, his tone shifting. "It was torture not being able to talk to you."

"I know... for me too," I reply as he pulls me in for another hug. "And when you and your mom came up to the hospital... I wanted so badly for them to leave us alone for even a minute."

"I was happy enough just seeing you in person... seeing with my own eyes that you were alive, even if we couldn't speak freely," he responds, causing me to blush.

"I'm truly sorry for what I did," I add. "For going to the cabin, especially without even letting you know. It all just happened so fast."

"I know you were just doing what you thought you had to... but next time, I'd appreciate it if you would include me in these life-threatening antics of yours," he says with a grin.

Though I try to resist, tears begin flowing freely down my cheeks and onto his t-shirt. He doesn't let go until I pull away.

"So, do you believe me?" I inquire hesitantly.

"*Believe?*" he asks, seemingly confused.

"You know—everything I saw that night inside Leon's cabin."

"Well, of course I do. You're not crazy, Greer. At least, not any crazier than me," he responds.

It feels as though a suffocating weight has been lifted from my chest as we both take a seat at the edge of the bed. *Thomas doesn't think I'm psychotic. Hallelujah.*

"It's just that… they didn't find anything the next morning. And my phone is missing, so I have no proof of anything," I say, looking to him for a reaction.

"Even with all that you went through, I think you'd know if it was real or not," he says reassuringly.

"Did you get to talk to the officers who searched the cabin?" I ask.

"No… your dad just let us know they didn't find anything except some furniture," he replies. "But I did look through the windows myself yesterday. The front door was locked. I… didn't see anything either. In fact, it looked really clean. I could see the light reflecting off the floors; not a speck of dust in sight," Thomas adds.

I lay my head back on the bed, feeling defeated. "I *know* someone cleaned it later that night… or early the next morning before the police made it there."

"But how would they know to take your phone?" he asks.

"I couldn't tell you," I respond, covering my face with a throw pillow. "They must have seen me go inside. I mean, that's the only way they'd know I'd taken pictures, right?"

Thomas nods in agreement, though we both know we can't really be sure of anything.

"Do you still think it's Leon?" I ask.

"I mean… he's the only person we know of with a grudge against the estate," he responds flatly.

"*I agree…* he's given us more than enough reasons to suspect him. Though I'm not sure he really has anything against Langley itself. *It seems to me that his issue is with my father… and with me,*" I add.

"But *why?*" Thomas asks.

"I suppose because we're outsiders to him… *and always will be.*"

"So, you're saying that Leon is a snob, *essentially?*" he quips, lightening the mood. "He thinks you and your dad aren't good enough for Langley Estates?"

"Yes, essentially," I reply. "Leon is the Marie Antoinette of our time."

Though we take a moment to enjoy the comic relief, I'm soon feeling once again low at the thought of all my efforts having been a complete waste of time. And not only that—but a waste which nearly cost me my life.

"We'll figure this out, Greer. I know we will," Thomas says as he grabs my hand. He's impressively attuned to shifts in my mood. It seems most guys I've known have a bit of difficulty in this area. At least, more so than women. My father has never excelled in the fine art of perception, so it's a nice change.

I'm sure Thomas can sense the weight of disappointment that I feel. We spend the next hour discussing every minute detail I can recall from the cottage that night. The mess. The photographs on the wall. The scribblings.

"So, the photos of all of us—were there any that only someone who knows us could have had access to?" Thomas asks.

"I don't think so," I reply.

"What about the photo of Leon?" he asks hopefully. "Has anyone ever posted a photo of him on social media?"

I pause a moment to think. The photo of Leon displayed in his former residence was pretty generic, from what I can remember. He was standing in front of Langley in his usual work clothes. He wore a very subtle smile on his face as he stood looking straight into the camera lens.

"Have you ever seen a photo posted of him *anywhere*?" Thomas probes.

"Well, now that you mention it… I don't think I *have*. The photo just didn't seem very personal. It was posed—almost like an employee photo or something."

"Obviously if Leon was the one staying there, he would have had plenty of photos of himself to choose from," he reasons.

"But why *would* he? To me it seemed like the photos, the map, the scribblings… they were all a part of some master plan. It was like we are *all* players in some game. Why would Leon have included *himself*?" I ask.

Thomas sighs. "I really don't know. I mean… maybe he wanted you to see it. Whether it's Leon or someone else, maybe they were luring you to the cabin that night by leaving all the lights on."

It was a thought I had not yet considered. What if I walked right into a trap? It would certainly explain how the perpetrator knew he needed to get the cabin cleaned up before police arrived, and that I had taken photos. But for what purpose? He could have grabbed me right then and there, yet didn't.

"Listen, Greer—I think you should take a break from thinking about all of this. Maybe something else will come to you later that can point us in the right direction," he says as he stands from the guest bed, offering his hands.

After helping me up, Thomas pulls me into a warm embrace. It feels good just to be back on my feet. It feels even better knowing I can, once again, speak freely with him whenever I wish.

As he begins to slowly release me from his arms, I take a small step back in order to look him in the eyes (probably the thing I missed the most while we were apart).

His face is sheer perfection. His eyes keep me captivated whilst in his presence. His lips draw me close like a magnet, unable to resist the pull.

He looks as if he wants to kiss me, but I beat him to the proverbial punch and move in closer until there is no space between us. Our lips lock together so naturally, as if we've been doing this for years. After experiencing such an intense amount of physical discomfort the night I lost consciousness in my bathtub, I never thought I could feel this good again. Yet here I am–tingling from head to toe and wishing this feeling never had to be forfeited.

Our kiss is more intense than before. I suppose living through a near-death experience is bound to yield a sense of urgency for a couple. I don't know about him, but I certainly thought for a time that we would never have this chance again.

After a few minutes, I finally manage to will myself into backing away from him. He greets me with the sweetest smile, revealing the dimple in his right cheek, as I once again meet his gaze.

"Oh, before I forget..." I say, whilst locating my new phone still resting on the bed behind me, "I really do need your phone number."

***

Thomas and I spend most of the day discussing recent happenings at the estate, no matter how hard we try to switch gears to more pleasant topics. He's been very attentive. It's apparent that the hospitalization really did a number on him... and it's impossible not to feel guilty about that. It was foolish on my part, and I hate that I allowed some creep to push me to a place of throwing all caution and self-preservation out the window.

Dad checks on me several times over the next few hours. Though he seemed pleasantly surprised that I had fixed myself up for the day, he reminded me to stay off my feet for the foreseeable future. Thomas was enlisted by his mother to travel back and forth between the kitchen and my room delivering drinks and snacks, which I feel certain he would have done regardless.

"I suppose I've officially lost all connection to my former life," I say as Thomas shuts his laptop. He's been taking a math quiz online for the past half an hour, while I kept busy familiarizing myself with my new phone.

"What are you talking about?" he asks, furrowing his brow.

"I mean that I've lost all my phone numbers. And it was difficult enough trying to keep in touch with my friends before."

Thomas frowns as he takes a seat at the foot of the bed. "All you need to do is make a post on social media letting your friends know you lost your contacts. Then they can text your new number," he says hopefully.

I nod, though feeling disheartened at the prospect of putting myself out there only to be let down by the response. Despite being used to the relative isolation of growing up without traditional schooling, I don't know that I've ever felt more alone—even despite my budding relationship with Thomas.

At times I've felt as though Langley were on my side, knowing I have its best interests at heart—knowing I want to preserve my aunt and uncle's legacy. Yet at other times it seems like Dad and I are nothing more than unwanted intruders. *Someone* out there certainly thinks so.

"Do you happen to know what we're having for dinner?" I ask, changing the subject in an effort to lift my mood.

"My mom is making a roast; and I think we're staying," he responds with a grin. "I hope you don't mind."

I roll my eyes before peeling off the several layers of blankets weighing me down in order to make my way over to the window seat.

"I'm glad you're feeling better," Thomas says before joining me at the opposite end of the window cushion. "You're very resilient, you know?"

"I'm not so sure that's true... *but thank you*," I respond.

"Well, just a few days ago you flirted with death... and now you're good as new."

"I wouldn't exactly say that–I'm still a little slow-moving. And... *flirted* with death? Is that really the best way to phrase it?" I ask in jest.

"Okay, point taken. Death never stood a chance against you," he says, moving closer to me.

I nervously direct my attention out the window in an effort to pretend I hadn't noticed his sudden change in proximity. Despite my desire for human connection, I'm inexplicably resistant to his advances (no matter how innocent they may be). I don't know what could have changed in the past several hours, nor why I'm suddenly feeling standoffish. Thankfully, Thomas seems to notice my hesitation and gives me the space I need.

I feel certain that my apprehension has nothing at all to do with Thomas. It's deep down in my gut. It's the feeling that nothing is right in the world–*my* world at least. I'm on edge–as though in a state of fight or flight, despite the lack of an imminent threat. It feels like everything is about to come to a head.

"What is it?" Thomas asks, a look of concern spreading across his face.

"It's… it's difficult to put into words. But I just don't feel safe in this house. The longer I live here, the more I feel like I'm losing my mind," I admit.

"Losing your mind? Greer, you've just been through a lot lately," he says warmly.

"I hate to say it, but maybe these experiences of mine have *never* been real," I respond, devastated at the thought. I place my hand over my face–too humiliated to look up.

"If none of it was real, then who killed our animals? Who trashed your painting?" he asks emphatically.

"I don't know," I reply, gazing once again at the earth down below the window.

"The guidance counselor at my school once talked to us about… well, traumatic experiences," he begins. "Apparently these experiences can affect people in different ways–ways you might not expect. And I'd say you've had enough trauma in your life to throw *anyone* off-kilter."

I manage to look up at him, meeting his eyes as he awaits my reaction to his words. However, I seem to have lost my ability to form a sentence.

"I'm not saying that you don't know what you saw," he continues, filling the silence. "I'm just suggesting that maybe the way you view the world is... tainted, or even skewed by your past experiences."

I pause for several moments to think as Thomas looks on in silence. "You might be right... I don't know what's real or not anymore," I say, defeated.

"Well, there's one thing I *do* know for sure..." he declares confidently.

"And what's that?" I ask in earnest.

"No matter what was real and what wasn't... we'll get it worked out," he says with a reassuring smile. "I think the first thing we should do is try to find Leon."

"*Really?* You... want to go looking for him?" I ask, surprised by his words.

"We need to know whether or not to continue down this rabbit hole. And if he's innocent... we can look in other directions," he offers.

I agree, and within fifteen minutes I'm sitting in the passenger seat of his car as Thomas drives toward the last place Leon was known to have been staying–the only hotel in town.

CHAPTER FOURTEEN

"Are you alright?" Thomas asks, glancing over at me from the driver's seat.

"I'd let you know if I wasn't. *Promise,*" I respond.

The air is growing heavier with every passing mile as we inch closer to the hotel. I have no idea what we might say to Leon should we actually succeed in tracking him down. There's simply no way to accuse someone of terrorizing your home without being confrontational. As much as I want answers, I'm dreading the possibility of seeing him again.

I also hate having to lie to Dad, but Thomas and I knew that he would never agree to me leaving the house—for *any* reason, let alone to track down Leon. I turned out the lights in my bedroom and shut the door before making it to the front porch undetected. Meanwhile, Thomas kept my father and Anne-Marie occupied in the kitchen. He told them that I wanted to take a nap before dinner.

Thomas decided to feign a sudden craving for hot apple cider. He knew good and well that we were completely out of cider packets. Anne-Marie, thankfully, agreed to him making a quick grocery store trip—which bought us some much-needed time.

"Would the hotel even be allowed to tell us if he's still there?" I ask doubtfully.

"I'm gonna say no, probably not," Thomas responds with a shrug. "But it's not like it's a Hilton. I mean, it has forty to fifty rooms... *max*. We might get lucky and catch him sitting at the bar or something," he adds hopefully. "I also know a few guys who graduated last year that work there... I bet they'd tell us something. A wink or a nod is all we'd need for confirmation."

"Yeah, *that* and a room number," I say emphatically.

"Like I said... it's not a twenty-story high-rise," he replies with a grin.

***

We arrive at The Blake Hotel in less than ten minutes—hardly enough time to mull over all the reasons why this is tremendously imprudent. My knees feel a little shaky as we make it to the sidewalk, which leads to the large double doors at the front entrance. Though I can tell my nerves are starting to set in, I feel certain that my recent near-death experience is mostly to blame for my current physical state. *I'm weak. And I'm exhausted.* I've put my young body through hell, and yet I continue to press on. The only thing that matters to me at this point is getting some answers.

If Leon *is* involved in sabotaging the estate, I have to know once and for all. If I've been seeing things that are not a genuine part of reality, I need to seek out some sort of help for myself. A doctor; a counselor—*someone*. Thomas wasn't wrong when he said I've endured more than my fair share of trauma.

The lobby of the hotel is tastefully decorated with a surprisingly modern assortment of colorful furniture. Flat-screen televisions are mounted along the walls, offering a focal point for the seating areas. And although Thomas was right about it being a smaller establishment, it's surprisingly upscale for a town with little tourist industry. I suppose I'd envisioned Leon staying at some place with stains on the carpets and a sign out front promoting *"ice cold air conditioning."* I would have thought The Blake was too fancy for his taste.

A young man with wavy, brown hair and a crisp uniform sits at the front desk, directly behind a desktop computer. I find myself impressed at the speed in which the keys of his keyboard are clicking away, as he stares intently at the screen. It's not until Thomas and I have made it to within a few feet of the desk that he is aware of our presence.

The employee smiles as he stands from his chair to greet us.

"Good evening, guys... how can I help... *Thomas!* Nice to see you, man. It's been a while," the young man says as Thomas reaches for his hand.

"It sure has, Liam," he responds. "This is Greer Tipton. She and her dad have been living at Langley since Mrs. Cece passed."

"It's nice to meet you, Greer. Were you kin to Mrs. Cecilia?" Liam asks warmly.

"She was my aunt," I answer proudly.

"She was really such a kind lady. Everyone in town loved her," he says, a hint of sadness in his voice.

As I thank him, I notice a middle-aged woman wearing the hotel uniform exiting one of the two elevators a ways behind the front desk. Thomas doesn't seem to notice her as he and Liam continue on with their conversation.

The lobby is practically barren apart from one older gentleman sitting alone at the hotel bar, which is located at the far end of the first floor—past the elevators. The employee seems to notice Thomas and I visiting with Liam, as she stares in our direction for a few seconds before turning the opposite way towards the bar area. I can hear her offer the patron a menu just as Thomas rests his hand on my arm, as though to subtly steer me back to their conversation.

I suddenly feel very conscious of the fact that Thomas and I are two teenagers alone together at a hotel, likely appearing to passersby as though we're trying to check in. My cheeks feel warm, though I smile and nod along as Liam fills Thomas in on what he's been up to since graduating from their high school the previous year.

"That's great they'll let you work around your class schedule," I hear Thomas say as I try to determine whether or not the female bartender is still looking in our direction.

"It's worked out really well so far," Liam adds, glancing over at me as though trying to include me in the conversation.

I manage a smile, though I feel somewhat ridiculous for not having thought through our plans for the evening a bit more.

"So… what are you up to this evening?" he asks, turning his attention back to Thomas.

Humiliation sets in as I consider what this guy *must* be thinking right about now. I'm desperately hoping that Thomas will, at long last, inquire about Leon so that we can get out of this lobby as soon as possible. My stomach drops as I watch an older couple exit the elevators and make their way past us towards the front entrance. I hang my head unnaturally low, feeling the weight of judgment bearing down on me, whether it be real or imagined.

"Well, the thing is…" Thomas begins hesitantly, "I was wondering if you've seen Mr. Leon around… you know, older guy–he's worked at the Langley Estate for ages."

"Oh yeah, I know Leon… he's been staying here for a while," Liam responds casually. "He's kind of hard to miss–he's a bit more… *earthy*… than our typical clientele."

Well, that's a way to describe a man who is perpetually disheveled that I haven't heard before.

"Yeah, that's what I'd heard," Thomas says coolly, though I can tell he's trying not to seem overly eager. "So, he's still here, then… hasn't checked out yet I mean?"

"Not that I know of," Liam replies.

"Well, Greer and I were kind of hoping we might run into him. There's just been some things going on at Langley and we… have been trying to get in touch,"

Thomas says, doing an impressive job at making this situation seem much less serious than it actually is.

A middle-aged woman with her hair swooped up in a bun is power-walking towards us from the opposite side of the lobby. She's already passed the elevators by the time I realize she's headed our way from the bar, where the older man once again sits alone.

"What can I help you two with this evening?" the employee asks sternly as she moves in next to Liam.

Thomas tries his best to exchange pleasantries, though he struggles to utter anything of substance as the woman crosses her arms, clearly waiting for a response to her inquiry.

"Good evening, ma'am," I begin, realizing quickly that I'll need to take over. "We were just trying to track down an old friend, and we'd heard he might be staying here."

"That's right," Liam adds. "Thomas was a classmate of mine. He and his friend were just hoping to see Mr. Leon."

The woman behind the counter looks intently at Thomas.

"Thomas… *Chambers?*" she asks suspiciously.

"Yes… I mean, yes ma'am," he replies nervously.

"I know your mother… Anne-Marie," she says, her face tightening.

"Oh, yes ma'am… that's her."

"I talk to her from time to time, hoping one day to persuade her to manage our housekeepers here at The Blake," the female employee adds flatly.

My eyes immediately settle on the gold name tag pinned to her uniform. It reads: "*Amelia Ponder - Manager.*"

"Ms. Ponder, I was just telling Thomas here…" Liam begins, trying to break the obvious tension that the hotel manager has brought to the conversation.

"I'm sure you were informing your friends, Liam, that we cannot release any information regarding possible guests of The Blake, as it is against company policy," she says plainly.

"Yes ma'am," Thomas chimes in, though a bit abruptly. "That's what Liam was just saying… but we appreciate your time nonetheless."

"It was nice meeting you, Liam," I say, smiling. "We'll be on our way now."

Liam reciprocates the sentiment as Thomas and I head towards the exit. Though Ms. Ponder remains silent, she stays firmly planted behind the check-in desk to keep an eye on us as we make it back to the parking lot.

Thomas and I don't exchange as much as a glance between us until we're back in the car.

"Well… that was a bust," he says once we're on the road, and a comfortable distance away from the hotel manager.

"I mean… not completely. Your friend Liam basically confirmed that Leon is still staying there… even if he wasn't really supposed to."

"True. But I sure do hope that woman believed Liam didn't tell us anything," he adds doubtfully.

"She didn't hear any of our conversation," I assure him. "And we covered for him. But… I *am* a little worried she might call your mom and tell her you were there tonight."

Thomas looks flushed as we pull into the grocery store parking lot. He's clearly worried.

"Why don't you just stay here and I'll go grab a box of cider real quick," he says, turning towards me. "There's no reason for you to get back out in the cold. In fact, I'm starting to regret getting you out of the house at all. You really should be resting… not dealing with this crap."

He leans back against the headrest, looking up at the ceiling before closing his eyes and taking a deep, purposeful breath. We both just sit for a while. *Quietly.*

Thomas and I are comfortable enough with one another to sit in complete silence. It never feels awkward or tense. Neither one of us is ever in a rush for the silence to end. No urgent need for it to be filled. We can just… *be.*

A few minutes pass before he opens his eyes.

"I'm sorry, Greer."

"You don't have anything to be sorry about," I say softly.

"It was my idea to look for Leon. I never should have got you out of the house. And I should have known it would be for nothing," he says, looking defeated. "It just seems like this guy is always two steps ahead of us. And what if you were to get hurt again? What if you didn't pull through next time?"

He pinches the space between his eyes as he lowers his head towards the steering wheel. His face is now red and blotchy, which he quickly wipes with his sleeve before a single tear is allowed to fall below his cheek.

"I really thought you were dead, Greer. And I hated myself for not stopping the person responsible in time," he continues.

"It's *my* fault I ended up in the hospital. No one made me do what I did–not even Leon *(or any other unidentified perp)*," I protest.

"It seems like there's only two ways that this can end, Greer. Either you or Owen get hurt. *Or* you have to leave the estate if it becomes too dangerous for you to stay."

I don't think I've fully appreciated what Thomas must have been feeling the other night, up until this moment. I also didn't realize how he'd blamed himself for it.

"Hey, I'm right here. And I'm not going anywhere," I say confidently. "Dad and I won't be run out of town by some sadistic coward."

My words seem to have done some good, as Thomas manages a smile before squeezing my hand. "I'll be back in a minute," he says before exiting the car.

***

As we make it back to the house, I quickly notice that Langley is lit up in the darkness like a torch.

"I'll take the cider to the kitchen, and come back for you once there's a clear path up to your room," Thomas says as we both exit the car.

"Do you think it's weird how all the lights are on?" I ask hesitantly.

He doesn't have a chance to respond before the front door flings open, revealing my father and Anne-Marie standing in the foyer. Neither of them look happy to see us. Thomas and I exchange a quick glance before climbing the steps to the front porch.

We both remain silent as we make it into the warm house. It's unclear if they had received a phone call revealing our whereabouts earlier in the evening, or if one of them discovered my absence on their own. Either way, there's no use in trying to cover for ourselves. In fact, it would probably just make everything worse, depending on how much they already know.

"Mr. Owen, I'm sorry I took Greer out. It was poor judgment on my part," Thomas says solemnly.

"What exactly did you think you were going to do if you'd succeeded in tracking down Leon?" Anne-Marie asks. Though she isn't raising her voice, her tone leaves me concerned for how the remainder of this conversation is going to go.

"Mom, I'm sorry. I... don't know what I'd planned on saying, really," he admits.

"Ms. Ponder at The Blake gave me a call, Thomas. It's not like you to lie," she says before taking the box of apple cider packets from his hands and leaving for the kitchen in frustration.

"You haven't been making the best decisions lately either, Greer. Why do you keep putting yourself in harm's way?" my father asks seriously.

"I don't mean to, Dad. We just want to settle this once and for all so we can live without having to fear this person."

"But that's *not* your job," he responds quickly. "And it's not *yours* either," he adds, looking over at Thomas. "I'm asking both of you right now to stop pushing this. Stop playing detective before you end up hurt again, or worse!"

Thomas and I both nod our heads in agreement.

"I'm sorry I scared you... *again*," I offer as my father makes eye contact with me.

"Well... how about we pick back up on this tomorrow, kids. For now, let's just enjoy the nice dinner Anne-Marie made for us," he says at last, leaving me feeling undeniably relieved.

Once seated at the kitchen table it seems as though everyone is making a genuine effort to move past the events of the evening. The mood is relatively lighthearted and normal–apart from the near-constant insistence that I remain seated at my chair.

"Thank you for making dinner, Anne-Marie. It's all so delicious," I say, as Thomas and Dad help themselves to more of everything.

"It was my pleasure. We're just so glad to have you home," she replies warmly.

"Though, in fairness…" Thomas chimes in. "Greer *has* been eating nothing but hospital food the past few days. It's not exactly a tough act to follow," he says, trying not to laugh.

"Um, excuse me–do you really want to play with me right now?" Anne-Marie replies in jest.

I'm relieved she seems to have softened up a lot since we first arrived back at the house. I don't want Thomas bearing the brunt of the blame for our actions. I could have said 'no' if I'd really wanted to, but the truth is that I'd do almost anything at this point to keep the estate from any further harm. What if Thomas is right about Dad and I having to leave eventually? What would happen to the employees? The estate? Aunt Cecilia's beautiful home?

"Have you had any updates from the police, Dad?" I ask.

"No, not today. They say they're working on it," he replies.

"What about patrolling?" Thomas interjects. "I didn't see anyone out there when we left earlier."

"The chief said they just don't have the manpower to be here 24/7, but they have someone drive by every hour or so," Anne-Marie replies, an air of disappointment in her voice. "I suppose *something* is better than nothing."

"Well, what about hiring private security, Mr. Owen?" Thomas asks, sounding a bit flustered by the news.

"I don't know about that, Thomas," my father responds. "We'll just see how it goes for now. And we *do* have Ben here during the day."

"Like we said before, try not to worry about anything. Owen and I have a handle on it," Anne-Marie adds.

Though I can tell he's not satisfied with that answer, Thomas manages to remain quiet and allow the conversation to move on from the topic. He and Dad soon begin clearing plates as Anne-Marie spoons leftovers into Tupperware bowls.

Though I'd offered to help, the best I could negotiate was being allowed to rest on the couch in front of the living room fireplace, rather than my bedroom. The fire is especially comforting tonight. I had really missed the way it crackles and pops with effortless fluidity during my nights spent away from Langley.

My hospital stay may have been the first time I'd ever really thought of Langley as home, and now that I've returned it feels better than ever to be here. I even feel a bit hopeful that perhaps we're in the clear. Apparently, there haven't been any more incidents since the night Dad and I left in an ambulance.

Before long, I'm joined by Thomas who brings with him two mugs of hot apple cider. He plays a few songs for me on his phone as we sit together on the couch, just as we've done so many times before.

"You know, I hardly ever listened to anything released past the early-2000s until I met you," I say before taking a sip of my drink.

"I'm well aware that you're a Martian," he quips.

"Well, it's tough *not* to be when you grow up the way I have," I reply, rolling my eyes at him.

"I'm glad you're home," he says seriously.

"I'm glad that... *you're* glad I'm home," I reply jokingly. "There was a time when I wasn't so sure you wanted to be here all the time."

"What do you mean?" he asks.

"Do you think you and I would have ever become friends at all if your mom didn't force you to be here while she's working?" I ask nervously.

He takes a moment to push the blonde hair from his forehead as he stares at me, seemingly amused.

"Come on, Greer. You're one of the most intelligent... *and perceptive* people I've ever met," he says plainly. "You haven't figured out by now that my mom does *not* make me come over here every day?"

"She... doesn't?" I ask, confused by his admission. "But you said..."

"I know that's what I told you, and I'm sorry about that. But I couldn't just *tell* you that I wanted to see you every day. I already had to deal with my mom and Ben giving me a hard time about it."

"They knew you wanted to see me?" I ask.

"I used to stop by a couple times a week after school, *until you moved in*. I mean, it was pretty obvious."

My face feels unnaturally tingly as I try my best to refrain from grinning like a fool. I've never imagined that our afternoons spent together meant as much to him as they have to me. I've had no prior experience with boys or dating. And I'm starting to recognize that my own insecurities have kept me from seeing what was right in front of me.

"I didn't know," I say softly, getting emotional.

"Can I kiss you now?" he asks, pulling me closer to him.

"Yes."

His lips touch mine just as he places his arm around my back. I've never felt more secure in my life.

Mere seconds pass before our time together is interrupted by the sound of a man's voice screaming into the darkness outside. I recognize instantly that the voice belongs to my own father, and that he's in pain.

CHAPTER FIFTEEN

"What is happening!?" Thomas asks, the terror apparent in his voice.

I run towards the kitchen as Thomas follows quickly behind. The door leading outside is already wide open upon our arrival. We reach the concrete steps. I try to make sense of what I'm seeing, though nothing seems to be registering.

My eyes need a few seconds to adjust before I realize that my father is involved in a physical altercation with another man. Dad is covered in blood. He and the perpetrator seem to be trying to wrestle one another to the ground with impressive force.

Anne-Marie emerges from inside the house, nearly knocking us over as she scrambles to make it down the steps and onto the dirt below.

"LEON!" Anne-Marie exclaims loudly.

Light from inside the house beams through the darkness via the open door. The two men inch closer to where we all stand, making their identities much easier to discern. *My father and Leon are engaged in an all-out brawl.*

Thomas steps forward as though he is going to intervene. That is until he is stopped cold by Anne-Marie, who has a firm grasp on his arm.

"No, Thomas. *No!* Get Greer inside and the two of you call 911. *NOW!*" she screams. Thomas quickly steps back into the kitchen and pulls his cell phone from his pocket. I stay firmly planted where I am—trying to decide what to do. I'm frozen—but not as a result of the weather.

My father and Leon are yelling loudly at one another in the midst of their scuffle, though their words are tough to make out. The blood covering Dad's face, hands, and chest seems to be originating from his nose. The two men are both coated heavily in dirt and snow.

"Leon! Stop! Leave!" Anne-Marie continues in vain.

"The police are on their way," Thomas says as he joins me once again on the cold steps.

I'm relieved when my father stands suddenly from the ground, though Leon is able to do the same just moments later. And as quickly as this all began, *it's over*. Leon stumbles backwards before falling abruptly to his knees. My father is standing perfectly still.

I notice a reflection in the darkness, close to Leon. He stares down as though in disbelief, placing his hand on the handle of a knife which is protruding from his stomach. I recognize it instantly as belonging to Leon himself—the same knife he always carries with him. The decorative pattern of the handle is very distinctive, and currently reflecting into the darkness like a beacon.

"He was... trying to kill me," my father says, stuttering. "He would have killed Greer."

Leon is on his knees, in shock and beginning to shake violently. He screams out in agony.

The sound of sirens pierces through the night air. Thomas runs toward the front of the house, waving his arms frantically. Paramedics are first on the scene, followed by no less than ten police vehicles.

Anne-Marie makes her way slowly over to my father, wrapping her arms around him. Meanwhile, Leon is transferred carefully onto a gurney by several medics, and subsequently loaded into the back of an ambulance.

Police swarm the estate. Nothing about this feels real. Thomas grabs my hand as we watch the scene play out in front of us. I suddenly realize that I'm barefoot, and also without a coat. Thomas seems to notice that I've begun to shiver and pulls me closer to him.

"You need to go inside and warm up," he says, looking worried.

"I can't leave my dad out here," I reply emphatically.

My father hasn't moved. Anne-Marie is comforting him—her arms still wrapped around his midsection. I start to consider going back inside the house, if only just to grab a coat and shoes. I'm sure it will take quite a while for police to gather witness statements, and there's no use in me ending up in the hospital again.

It is just when I turn towards the door at the top of the steps that I hear a voice I recognize. It's Officer Hank, who is walking hurriedly toward my father and Anne-Marie.

"*Owen Tipton*," Hank says sternly. "You're under arrest. Place your hands behind your back."

This can't be real. Am I having a nightmare? Am I having some kind of stress-induced hallucination!? I look over at Thomas and squeeze his hand, just to help convince myself that I'm even standing here on these steps right now.

Officer Hank places my father in handcuffs as a stunned Anne-Marie stands watching in disbelief.

"Wait… Hank," she says frantically. "It was self-defense! Leon attacked him! He's obviously the person who has been harassing us all this time; the one who killed our animals!" she protests.

Hank seems to be doing his best to tune her out as he escorts my father towards the front of the house. Thomas and I follow after them as Anne-Marie continues to try to get through to Hank.

"Officer, please just wait! Please let us tell you what happened," I cry out in desperation.

He finally pauses briefly to look over at me, with one hand holding on to the cuffs behind my father's back, and the other placed between his shoulder blades. Dad stares at the ground as though in a trance.

"*Greer*," Hank begins, as if he's still contemplating whether or not to respond. "Your father is under arrest for the murder of your Aunt Cecilia."

***

Thomas helps me inside the house after we watch from the front porch as Hank's patrol car disappears into the darkness. I could see Dad sitting in the backseat as they ventured down the long driveway, yet he never turned around to look back at us. A light must have been on inside the vehicle, as I could see the back of his head clearly slumped forward. He never uttered as much as a single word to anyone after he was cuffed. It's difficult for me to even reconcile with the fact that it was truly him—*my dad*—removed from our family home as an accused murderer.

Anne-Marie and Thomas do everything they can to make me comfortable in the informal living room. Physically, I feel terrible. *Miserable*, in fact. I'd spent an extended period of time outside in the cold (in improper clothing, no less) while still recovering from hypothermia. I looked on as my father seemingly fought for his life, and subsequently witnessed a stabbing just feet from where I stood. Then in an unexpected turn—my only surviving parent, my caregiver, *my dad* has been falsely accused of killing his own aunt.

I'm covered in several layers of blankets by Anne-Marie, as Thomas runs upstairs to fetch some warm clothes. The couch seems to swallow me whole as I stare blankly at the TV, frozen with fear and trepidation. I've never felt more lost.

"How could they possibly think he killed Cece?" I blurt out as Thomas slips a pair of thick socks on my feet. Anne-Marie is sitting on the rug in front of the couch. I can tell that her mind is racing, but she's trying to distract herself by focusing her attention on me.

"I'm not sure, sweetheart," she replies solemnly.

"What if Leon framed him? What if this was his way of getting rid of Dad after nothing else worked?" I ask as warm tears begin streaming down my face.

"But if that was his plan then why would Leon show up here and attack him? Why not just let him go to jail?" Thomas asks tentatively.

Nothing makes any sense anymore. The three of us sit together with the TV playing quietly in the background. My body warms slowly under the blankets, though I find it difficult to stop shivering. In a way, my physical discomfort is a welcome distraction from the current reality that I find myself in.

A sudden knock at the front door echoes through the house like a fire alarm. The three of us exchange glances before Anne-Marie instructs Thomas and I to stay put in the living room.

Thomas grabs his cell phone from the coffee table as I push myself up into a seated position.

"Do you need another pillow?" he asks.

"No, I'm okay. But thank you for… everything. I honestly don't know what I would do if you and your mom weren't here."

"Greer, you don't have to say thank you. I mean, where the heck else would I be?" he asks, seemingly doing his best to lighten the mood.

Anne-Marie soon returns, followed by Ben who's looking especially grave. He is joined by an older gentleman that I don't recognize. He is dressed in a dark charcoal suit and shiny dress shoes. His gray hair is tastefully styled, highlighting a few streaks of black throughout.

"Greer, are you okay?" Ben asks.

"No… *But*, I'm glad you're here," I reply.

Ben nods. "I'd like to introduce you to someone. This is Mr. Ronald–he and his wife are our neighbors across the street," he says, gesturing towards the man in the suit.

"It's nice to finally meet you, my dear," Mr. Ronald says. "Your aunt and uncle always spoke so highly of you. And I had a chance to get to know Frank a bit as well during his time here–and I have to tell you, he was one *proud* grandfather."

"It's nice to meet you as well. Though, I'm afraid you're not catching me on my best day," I reply.

"Yes, dear. *I know*," he whispers softly.

"*Ben*, Mr. Owen has been arrested," Thomas interjects. "They think he *killed* Mrs. Cece! And Leon showed up here tonight, and…" he continues, but is cut off by Ben.

"Thomas, Thomas… It's okay. *I know*. I know everything," Ben says, looking downcast. "Ronald and I have just come from the police station."

"But *why?*" I ask, though I'm not certain I can survive another shock to the system today.

"Well, if I may," Mr. Ronald begins, as both he and Ben take a seat in nearby armchairs. "I'd like to offer my condolences on the deaths of your aunt and grandfather. You see, my wife and I have been traveling abroad for the past several months, and only just returned home this week. So, I've only just learned of their passing."

"Oh, I see," I reply. As though I didn't feel sick enough before, the anxiety I'm currently experiencing in anticipation of where this is all going has me wondering if I should ask Thomas to grab a trash can from the kitchen. This nausea just might get the better of me.

"Your Mr. Leon—I've known him for many years. Well... he paid me an unexpected visit at the house yesterday. Apparently he'd asked our housekeeper to let him know once we'd returned," Mr. Ronald continues.

I remain stoic as he speaks, though my stomach turns at the mention of Leon's name.

"You may have noticed that we have a lot of security cameras along our front gate and fencing," he says, glancing over at Ben before continuing. "Well, Leon was very anxious to review my security footage—specifically the time period leading up to Cecilia's death."

Mr. Ronald clears his throat. It seems he's having a hard time making it through what he came here to say.

"So, he and I sat down to comb through the footage together. Leon said we were just looking for anything out of the ordinary. *Well...* on December 23rd, the night before the wreck—we spotted a man sneaking onto Langley, through the front gate."

"*Greer,*" Ben interjects. The tone in his voice causes literal pain in my gut. I've never seen him as serious as he is right now. "Leon recognized the man who trespassed onto the property—*it was Owen.* It was your father. He must have parked his car a ways back, because he was on foot when he made it to the front gate. This... was at about three in the morning."

I try to speak, yet find myself incapable of uttering even a single word. I feel like a mere shell of a person and nothing more. *Hollow.*

"So, Leon and I took the footage to the police station yesterday evening to see what they could make of it," Ronald says hesitantly. "Leon was… *furious.* He wanted to confront Owen, but the chief and I convinced him to give them a chance to look into it. And… possibly make an arrest."

Anne-Marie and Thomas look gutted, though they both continue to glance over at me every few seconds as though I might shatter before their very eyes.

"Leon and Mr. Ronald called me earlier today and asked if I would meet them at the police station," Ben interjects. "The officers let us know that they located Mrs. Cece's car in the junkyard. We didn't know if it would even still be there… *but*, they were able to take a look at it. They… didn't have a reason at the time of the crash to believe her death was anything more than a terrible accident."

Ben looks like he has just run a marathon. *He's pouring sweat.* I notice his hand shaking uncontrollably as he places it at his forehead, taking a moment to shut his eyes.

"*Greer*," Ben continues, following a pregnant pause. "The hydraulic brake lines of your aunt's car had been cut. After she left the house on Christmas Eve, she would have kept picking up speed until she busted through the railing of the embankment. As you know, it's downhill, and… she didn't have any brakes. *Someone wanted her to crash.* And, the police believe that Owen was the person who tampered with her car… the night before the wreck."

"After the police let us know they had enough to make an arrest, Leon stormed out of the station," Ronald adds, looking over at Ben. "We tried to stop him. *But,* he was inconsolable once he learned what had been done to Cece's car. He was… out of his mind with rage. We knew he was going to confront Owen. I just… *still can't believe he's been stabbed,*" he says solemnly. "The police were just minutes behind him, on their way to make the arrest."

CHAPTER SIXTEEN

The next morning, Anne-Marie informed us that the police called to say they would be stopping by Langley to take statements. None of us slept after Mr. Ronald left late last night. Ben, Anne-Marie, and Thomas all stayed over. I remained on the couch as though it were my final resting place.

After our conversation last night, I tried to ask questions—but I could tell that Ben really wanted to give me a break before bombarding me with any new information. There's nothing that anyone can say to make this better for me. I would say I'm living a nightmare, but of all the loss I've experienced throughout my life—I never could have fathomed losing this much.

Thomas kept the TV on throughout the night and early morning. I spent several long stretches of time staring blankly at the screen, though I wouldn't categorize it as actually watching TV. It was more so a tool used to help guide me into a trance-like state. All I desired was temporary respite from my emotions. *A numbness.*

I want to speak with Ben privately before the police get here this morning. I haven't yet come close to accepting the version of events that were presented to me last night. There has to be some kind of mistake. Some explanation for all of this. If Leon is an innocent party then there would have to be someone still out there who has made it their mission to terrorize the estate and run us off. *Someone* had to have killed the animals. *Someone* had to have threatened us, along with trashing the garage storage closet.

"Ben?" I say tentatively.

"Hey," he replies, seemingly a bit startled as it's the first words out of my mouth in at least a couple of hours. "Do you want me to get you something from the kitchen? Anne-Marie and Thomas are making some breakfast."

"No, *thank you though*. I'm… wondering if we can talk… while the two of them are busy."

He nods and takes a seat across from the couch.

"I've been thinking a lot, and I'm wondering if anyone else identified my dad on Ronald's security video. I mean… Mr. Ronald has never met my father. *What if it wasn't him?* You said this happened at three in the morning—*how much of this person's face can be seen on the video?*" I ask doubtfully.

Ben takes a few moments before responding. I can tell he is choosing his words carefully.

"As far as the security footage goes—I haven't seen it myself because I wasn't there when Leon and Mr. Ronald initially spoke to the police and handed over the video. I assume that the police reviewed the tape and agreed that it was, in fact, Owen on the grounds that night. *But*, obviously I can't say for certain," he offers.

"So, all we really know is that *someone* tampered with Cece's car the night before the wreck. We don't know for sure that it was Dad. *What if Leon is trying to frame him?* How do we know it isn't Leon himself on the security footage?" I press.

"I… I don't know, Greer. Leon handed the video over to the police. *Mr. Ronald was with him.* It's just hard for me to believe that they would arrest Owen if they couldn't positively ID him on the video. *But… when the chief gets here I'm sure he could answer that for you."*

"Ben, we know for a fact that Leon was dragging Dad's name through the mud all over town. I heard those ladies at the nail salon say so!" I protest. "Leon hates my father. He's done everything in his power to get rid of him."

"But…" Ben responds carefully. "If your Aunt Cece were still alive, Owen never would have taken over Langley in the first place. *Leon had no reason to want Cece dead.* He… he loved her. And he spent many happy years taking care of the estate. I mean, he's always been a bit of a pain. But he was happy here… *with her."*

I can feel the frustration rising up inside of me. Ben isn't even listening. He doesn't understand that Dad *couldn't* have done this. *He's not a killer. He's just not!*

"Sweetheart…" Ben continues. "Leon and I spoke soon after he was fired. He confided that he'd always had suspicions your aunt's wreck was not an accident. He… said she'd asked him to bring her some firewood the night of the crash. The two of them were in the living room talking when she got a phone call," he says before taking a deep breath. "She never drove after dark. She hadn't for years. But she ran out of the house that night after taking that call. Leon said she was completely frazzled. Hysterical, even. He asked her what was wrong, but she just… told him she didn't have any time to explain. That it was an emergency. *She died minutes later."*

"Did he know *who* she'd been talking to?" I ask.

"*No*. And of course she took her cell phone with her when she left. To our knowledge it has never been recovered," Ben replies.

"But, what about phone records?"

"When Leon learned that she had passed away, he was a mess. He was completely out of his mind with grief. He, *like all of us*, had no reason to suspect any sort of foul play. The driving conditions were bad, and she *never* drove after dark. So when the police determined she'd hydroplaned, none of us had any reason to question it. *But*... Leon couldn't stop thinking about that phone call. *He*... said he didn't think that it would be enough though for the police to get involved," Ben says solemnly. "I told you before that he drove to the crash site the day after she died–*Christmas Day,* and I had to pull his truck out of a ditch after he ran off the road," he continues. "Leon couldn't find any skid marks on the road where she would have tried to stop the car. And he *knew* that there should have been no issues with her brakes. You might recall that Leon was the one to take care of the vehicle for her. He was downright religious about the maintenance schedule for that car of hers."

"But, again... if there were no skid marks–why didn't he talk to the police?" I ask, growing increasingly agitated. I suddenly realize my breathing has been unnaturally shallow for the past several minutes, and as a result I've become a bit lightheaded.

"Are you doing okay, Greer?" Ben asks, concerned.

"*Yes*," I reassure him, pausing for a moment to take several deep breaths, though it does very little to help.

"Leon didn't take his suspicions to the police because he knew they'd have said any evidence of skid marks would be buried in snow and ice," Ben continues.

"*Okay*... but why would Leon destroy my painting? Why would he have killed our animals!?"

Ben looks at me with such dread in his eyes. I know he wishes we didn't have to continue, because I wish the same. But we both know that we don't have that luxury.

"Greer, he didn't... *he didn't do any of it.* We... believe that it was all your father's handiwork. He was trying to frame Leon so that he could get rid of him. So that he could get him away from Langley."

"You don't know that, Ben! You *can't* know that!" I exclaim in protest. Tears quickly begin to flow as I am no longer able to maintain my composure. "You're asking me to accept that my own father is a cold-blooded murderer who killed Aunt Cece for, what? *Money I guess.* What else!?" I scoff in disgust.

"No, sweetheart. *No.* I'm not asking you to take in all of this in one day and just accept it as truth. *No one expects that.* I'm just telling you what I know. And... I honestly can't imagine the pain you're in," he says, his own eyes filling with tears.

"If what you're telling me *is* true—my dad would have had to call Cece the night of Christmas Eve... before he and I sat down to dinner. And... what? Told her *something* that would have caused her to immediately jump in her car—knowing she would have no brakes? Knowing she shouldn't be driving after dark? Knowing the roadways were covered in snow and ice!?"

Ben looks on from his armchair as I stand to my feet in frustration and begin pacing quickly around the room. "So when Dad got the phone call that Cece had been in an accident—you're saying it was all an act?" I press. "You're saying he wasn't upset or scared or heartbroken like I was that night? He was just... sitting down to dinner with me waiting for a phone call that he KNEW was coming!?"

I can't stop crying. *Wailing,* in fact. I can hardly breathe. I'm suffocating. I'm screaming. I'm trying to wake myself up from this nightmare. I cover my midsection with my trembling arms, though I can't say *why*. I dig my fingernails into my skin just above the hips, yet hardly feel a thing. I want to throw up. I *need* to throw up. I am going to pass out if I don't sit down!

Falling to my knees, someone immediately wraps their arms around my body and pulls me against their chest. *Thomas is carrying me back to the couch.* Ben is standing close by, as is Anne-Marie. They are all crying, yet looking at me as though I'm the only person in the world that matters.

CHAPTER SEVENTEEN

It has been one week since my father was arrested and charged with the murder of my aunt. I've had more support in the past seven days than at any other time in my life. Anne-Marie, Thomas, and Ben have stayed with me around the clock. Ben's mother, Cora, has filled our kitchen with delicious casseroles and treats. They have all been so incredibly patient with me—so understanding. *So empathetic.*

Leon remains in the hospital, but is expected to recover. Ben and Anne-Marie have both visited him several times. Apparently our neighbor Mr. Ronald, along with his wife, sent a giant cookie basket to his hospital room, which I'm told he was particularly enthused about.

"Greer, are you ready?" Anne-Marie asks, standing in the doorway of my bedroom.

"I'll be right down," I reply, following a brief pause.

Though it's clear she was using the word *'ready'* in a very literal sense (as in hair and makeup done; clothes and shoes on), my initial instinct was to consider whether or not I am, in fact, *ready* to face the world outside the walls of Langley Estates again. The answer to *that* question is (unfortunately) much more complicated than whether or not I've fixed myself up to the point of being ready to leave the house for an outing.

Today is the first opportunity I've had in the past week to dress in clothing that is *neither* sweats, nor pajamas. I've opted for a blue dress, fun printed tights, and a yellow jacket warm enough to withstand the cold. Anne-Marie helped me blow-dry my hair after I took a much-needed hot shower this morning. It really is amazing what a bit of body wash and shampoo can do for one's emotional well-being.

Despite the excruciating mental toll that this past week has taken, I've made a very conscious effort to do everything within my power to recover physically, following my brush with death at the hands of the elements. I haven't stepped foot outside in days. I've stayed hydrated. I've done all that I can to ensure my health, especially considering the obstacles I will face moving forward. *I need to be at my best.*

Anne-Marie and Thomas are taking me to the hospital to visit Leon this morning. I've spent the past week asking more questions than at any other time in my life. I've also had a lot of time to think—*about my father*, and all that he has done. I started keeping a journal, trying my best to document every lie he has ever told me—*though I know the list will never be complete.*

I thought that my life was defined by death, but as it turns out—it was defined by the deception of one man, the person I loved and cared for the most. I had never questioned him. I thought that I knew him so well when— in actuality—I had only encountered a carefully-crafted version of him. A version he worked hard to convince those around him was his true and authentic self. He was very, very good at keeping up the facade.

I spent my adolescent life believing that all of my father's time spent away from home could be attributed to nothing more than his dedication to providing a good life for us. Yet I've now come to the realization that it is highly likely his absence over the years was due mostly to his desire to conceal his true self. I may never know *where* he spent his time whilst 'traveling for work,' nor do I *need* to know. Should I choose to chase down every rabbit hole left in my father's wake, I fear I run the risk of losing myself in the process.

The grief I feel for the loss of Grandpa Frank is more palpable and painful than ever. I'm left wondering what suspicions, if any, that he may have had. And I appreciate now, more than ever, his willingness to step up as my primary caregiver. He demonstrated love, empathy, and honesty every single day that he and I spent together.

***

The hospital aesthetic is even colder than I remember from my own stay not long ago. I've asked Anne-Marie and Thomas to give me some time alone with Leon before joining us in his room. I imagine that Thomas is already working on his second candy bar from the waiting room vending machine by now.

The room is quiet as I enter. I spot Leon playing solitaire from his hospital bed, though he hasn't yet noticed my presence. He looks somewhat different from the Leon I knew, though I can't put my finger on any particular reason.

"Mr. Leon," I whisper softly, hoping not to startle him. "May I come in?"

He looks up from his card game–his eyes catching mine.

"*Yes*," he responds, attempting to straighten out his hospital gown.

I take a seat at the armchair closest to the bed. He looks as calm as I've ever seen him, albeit a bit serious. He doesn't look nearly as intimidating as before–yet I still struggle with how to begin.

"I'm… *very sorry*, for everything," Leon says warmly.

"You… *are*? Sorry for what?" I ask, genuinely flabbergasted.

"For the way I've treated you since you first arrived at the estate. It was *never* about you, Greer. I was just… so angry."

"You were angry that Cece was gone. And you suspected my father was the one responsible?" I ask hesitantly.

"*Yes*," he responds, hanging his head.

"You had a right to be angry. *I'm* sorry that I suspected you of… well, *everything*."

Leon grins. "Well, in fairness, I haven't been the most pleasant person to be around. I'd probably have suspected me, too."

We both chuckle at the thought.

"But, may I ask you something?" I continue.

"Anything," he replies.

"There was this one night when the power was going out at Langley. I ended up running around the house because I could have sworn I saw you peering into my dad's bedroom window. But then, you were just… gone. *Am I crazy?*"

Leon shakes his head. "No, dear. You're not crazy. And I'm very sorry that I scared you. It was never my intention. But… you're correct. I *was* trying to spy on him that night. I was always fishing for… *something.* Anything that might point to his guilt. I combed through every piece of his mail that I could get my hands on. I was… desperate to know the truth."

"I understand," I respond, feeling a small sense of relief. "But, did you come inside the house? When I made it back upstairs there was a light left on in one of the bedrooms."

"No, I didn't," he replies, shaking his head gently.

"I suppose it was just me then. I must have turned it on when I was running from room to room, trying to keep up with you," I tell him.

"It was my fault, Greer. Anyone would have been paranoid under the circumstances."

"It's really okay," I respond, trying to reassure him that I now understand the position he was in.

"I didn't have access to the security video at that time… not until Ronald returned home. So, at that point, it was just a… a hunch, a feeling… that your aunt's wreck was no accident."

"But, why him? What made you suspect that it was my father?" I ask earnestly.

"Besides the fact that he was set to inherit millions of dollars?" he quips.

"Besides *that*," I reply, a bit shocked that Leon actually has a lighter side to him.

"It was the phone call she took on Christmas Eve. She'd asked me to bring her some firewood. We were just talking when she got the call," he says before tilting his head away from me slightly, as though trying to prevent himself from getting emotional. "I had never seen her so upset. I remember her asking the caller if 'she' was okay... then she hung up, and ran out the door."

"She asked: '*is she okay?*'"

"Yes," he replies. "It seemed like the caller had told her there was an accident of some kind. I... thought it might have been Owen who called, and told her that you had been hurt. It would explain why she was so frantic, and why she would have ventured out onto the roads that night. But of course, I'll never know for sure that it was your father."

My heart nearly pounds out of my chest as I search for the right words.

"Yes, Mr. Leon. He *was* the caller that night. *It was Owen.*"

"*What?* How do you know?" he asks, clearly shaken.

"After Ben told me that Cece had received an upsetting phone call that night, I asked the police chief if they could look into the cell phone records. *It was him.* My father spoke to her minutes before she got into her car and crashed."

Leon begins to sob.

"He had tampered with her car the night before," I continue. "He was... most likely just waiting for a phone call with news of her passing. *But* she didn't get out of the house that day. *So, he called her.* He called her and told her something that would make her get in her car and leave."

"*Yes,*" he replies, taking some time to regain his composure.

"Dad and I had visited Cece the night before she died," I add, wondering if Leon will be able to continue. "I wanted to bring her a Christmas present."

He nods.

"Aunt Cece and my father spoke privately that night. And when they returned... Cece seemed really upset. At the time, I just assumed it had to do with my Grandpa Frank. His death was still so raw," I say, leaning forward and resting my elbows on my legs. "Did my aunt ever... did she happen to tell you what they talked about that night?"

Leon clears his throat before responding. I can tell that what he has to say will be difficult to hear.

"*She did.* She... said that Owen asked for money. And she wouldn't give him any more," he replies.

"*Any more?*"

"Yes. Your father had been taking money from her for years. And, Cece had a hard time saying 'no.' She never even told Frank that she was helping to financially support his son. I don't think he would have allowed it."

"And with Frank being the beneficiary of Langley..." he continues. "I think your father was counting on inheriting it after his dad was gone. But of course, none of us expected that Frank would pass first. That night, Owen pressed her on whether or not he would be named beneficiary when she updated her will. She told him she *couldn't*. I'm not sure what her plans were exactly–Frank had just passed and she was still grieving. But she told your father she couldn't trust him with the estate. She loved Langley... and it was very important to her that it remain intact. That it be managed well."

"So, you're saying that Cece told him he would not be named beneficiary, and later that same night he made certain that she would pass away before having a chance to update her will? *Knowing that he would be her next of kin*," I ask, utterly devastated at each and every fact that comes to light.

Leon nods, shifting his eyes toward the floor in despair. "She'd been telling me about their conversation just before she got the call."

"You know, my father was hardly ever home–not until we moved to Langley. He was always traveling for work–or so he said. Who knows if any of what he said was true. Did he even have the job he said he did?" I ask rhetorically.

"The police chief told me that killing animals is something that's seen a lot in sociopaths, especially when they're young," I continue. "I remember Grandpa telling me years ago that they'd had a string of 'bad luck' with pets when my father was a child. Of course, I didn't make anything of it at the time. Why do you think he killed the animals at Langley?"

"To tell you the truth…" Leon begins. "I was trying my best to make his life at the estate as difficult as I could. I bad-mouthed him all over town. I suppose my goal was for him to slip up in some way. And… it seems as though I succeeded. There would have been plenty of opportunities for your father to poison the food, or their water. It's not as if Ben and I could be around 24/7. *The animals are dead because I pushed Owen to his limits.* And I feel terrible that I played a role in it."

"You couldn't have known what he would do," I reply, hoping to comfort him. "Is that why you stayed inside your cabin that day?"

"Yes, *it is,*" he responds. "I was the first to find them that morning–well before Anne-Marie arrived. I knew immediately who was responsible. I felt… sick (*that much was true*). And as luck would have it, I had already told Ben the night before I thought I could use a rest. I think it was the stress getting to me. So when I woke up to that the next morning, it felt almost like divine intervention that I had an excuse not to have to face it. I couldn't have faced your father that day; I wouldn't have been able to control my anger. I needed the day to cool off and just be alone."

"But, how did you hurt your hand? It was bandaged the next day," I ask.

"I fell and cut it on my old coffee table… just like I told you," he says, looking amused. "Not everything you've ever been told is a lie, Greer."

"Well… it's kind of hard to tell anymore," I reply, defeated.

"I felt terrible when I heard your painting had been destroyed. I regretted trying so hard to get under his skin. But I think his objective was always to get rid of me. He knew I was on to him. And blaming me for all the vandalism at the estate was the way to do it," he adds.

"Leon, I'm so sorry. You've been loyal to Langley for so long, and this is how you're rewarded," I reply, looking down at the bandaging covering his stomach. "I don't know how everything is going to work moving forward… seeing as how I'm not of legal age yet. But, if it's up to me, I'd really like for you to come home."

His eyes once again fill with tears. "I would love to," he replies softly.

"We have your truck parked in the garage for you. Ben said you'd just got it out of the shop a few days before you drove to the house that night."

"Yep. I *told* Ben he bent one of my tie rods when he pulled me out of that ditch," he says, rolling his eyes.

"*Leon*… could I ask you one more thing?"

"Shoot, kid."

"Were you in love with Cece?" I ask.

"*Yes*," he replies flatly and without hesitation, as though he has waited a lifetime to be asked that question.

"Did… she know?"

"I think she must have had an inkling. Women are very perceptive, you know. But, if you're asking me if I ever told her how I felt—*no*, I did not."

"*But...* Uncle Carl passed away years ago. *Why didn't you?*" I press.

"I... *thought I had more time*, I suppose. She was my closest friend," he says with a smile that tells me he will cherish every moment shared between them for the rest of his life.

"I know how much she appreciated you, Leon. *You took good care of her.*"

"Thanks, kid," he replies warmly. "She loved you, Greer. And she would be proud of the way you've handled yourself. *None of us have lost as much as you.*"

THE BIOGRAPHER

There hasn't been a lot of quiet in my life since having children. Yet as I sit across from the biographer, my home is uncharacteristically still. Sadie seems to be hanging on my every word—hardly even taking notes anymore. I can't recall the last time I would have spoken about this to such an extent. It's kind of surreal to revisit this part of my life, especially when I've worked so hard for so long to leave it behind me.

"What happened to your father?" Sadie asks tentatively.

"Owen accepted a plea bargain. The prosecutor took the death penalty off the table and he pled guilty to murder in the first degree," I respond. "Going to trial would have been completely asinine. There was just too much evidence. He was, as they say, *guilty as sin.*"

"Can I assume that Owen was the person who trashed Leon's cabin?" she asks.

"*Yes.* I suppose he was using it as his... *headquarters?* I'm not sure what to call it. He had photos of all of us pinned to the walls (*including himself*). There were the incoherent scribblings. The mess. It was all indicative of a person who was very unwell."

"But, how did he make it back in time to clear everything out before the police got there? Wasn't he at the hospital with you?" she asks curiously.

"I wondered that, too," I reply. "Eventually I had a chance to speak with the chief of police, and I asked him what time his officers made it to the cabin the morning after I'd discovered its contents, *(and ended up with hypothermia)*. I told him that my father made the call right in front of me in my hospital room. The chief told me that they never received a phone call from Owen about the cabin. So, he would have had plenty of time to clear it out, because he never actually made that call. I told Dad exactly where I'd left my phone, containing all the photos. Then all he had to do was tell us that nothing had been found. He... did a fantastic job at making me question my own sanity. I really thought I had lost my mind–that I was having hallucinations. That I was seeing things that weren't there."

"Wow, that's... a pretty egregious thing to do to someone–especially your own child," Sadie responds.

"Yes, it was. But at least I made it out alive," I say plainly.

"Yes. That you did," Sadie replies, wearing a sympathetic grin. "Did you ever see him again? *Owen?*"

"Only once."

CHAPTER EIGHTEEN

Six months have passed since my father was sentenced to life in prison. It has taken some time for me to come to terms with the fact that my life with Owen was all a lie. *Nothing* with him was what it seemed to be, and in the blink of an eye I lost every ounce of stability I had left.

I've come to the difficult decision to visit him before he will be moved to another penitentiary several hours away. Though I have no desire to maintain contact with him, there are a few things I would like to know before I close this chapter.

Owen and I are separated by a thick layer of plexiglass, making it necessary for old-school telephones to be utilized in order for us to communicate with one another. The temperature of the visitors' room is nothing short of freezing–and the cold, metal stool they have me seated on certainly isn't helping.

It seems as though all light and warmth abandoned this place long ago. Many of the inmates wear heavy chains around their hands and feet. Their expressions are lifeless and without hope. The images of these men being held captive like wild animals is much more painful to witness than I could have imagined.

The man staring back at me is not the father I once knew. He is a mere shell of a human being. His eyes are dark and empty. His skin is pale. He's lost at least twenty pounds since the last time we laid eyes on one another.

This place is where a man like Owen belongs.

"*Greer?*" he says, placing the phone to his ear.

"I have something I want to ask you," I reply.

"Okay."

"What did you say to Aunt Cece the night of the crash? What did you say to make her leave home?" I ask earnestly.

"Greer, I want you to understand something…" he begins.

"*No!*" I interject. "Don't do that! I didn't ask *why* you did what you did. I already know *why*. The only thing I *don't* know is what you said to her on the phone that night."

"I… said what I had to say," he responds, emotionless.

My throat is tightening, but I absolutely refuse to cry in front of this man. He will only perceive crying as weakness; and he will think he still holds some degree of power over me. I refuse to give him that satisfaction.

"*Fine,*" I say in disgust. "If you won't tell me what you said to Cece, will you *at least* tell me what you said to my mother? Before you drugged her and placed her in that bathtub?"

He pauses, though his face remains expressionless.

"*No,*" he responds coolly.

I've had enough.

"Okay, Owen. *Goodbye.*"

I know for certain that I will never see him again. Yet, as I walk swiftly towards the exit door, *I never think to look back.*

***

Ben's mother, Cora, has been named my legal guardian, seeing as how I have no close relatives—and all of my extended family lives clear across the country. I'm set to officially inherit the estate once I turn eighteen. In the meantime, Cora and Leon have been appointed co-managers of Langley.

Ben is now living at their family home on his own, while Cora moved into the estate with me. Despite all that has happened, the house now feels like home. Since Owen left, it's as though a weight has been lifted from the grounds. Light has found its way back into every corner—especially once Anne-Marie removed my father's belongings from his former bedroom.

Leon returned to his cabin. And with his newly-acquired duties as co-manager, he has officially passed the proverbial baton over to Ben with respect to the day-to-day tasks of the property. One of Ben's first acts as the sole groundskeeper was to, once again, fill the yard, chicken coop, and pens with farm animals.

Leon has been able to take over the business side of the estate and investments with relative ease, though he insisted that Aunt Cece's CPA, Rory, be hired to oversee it all. I can tell how much it means to him to maintain the integrity and legacy of Cece's home, even if it means taking on a 'desk job,' as he puts it.

I hope to attend art school out of state once I turn eighteen, and have completed my bachelor's degree. I can't allow my father's sins to define the rest of my life, and I'm afraid if I remain in this town, I will never escape my family's dark history.

Owen was not at all who I believed him to be, and his lies have continued to come to light since his arrest. His manipulations were chronic, and they were detrimental to everyone around him—*especially to me.*

I can look back now and see the ways in which he manipulated his own father. And yet, no matter what Grandpa Frank may or may not have suspected, he was never going to abandon me. His warmth and presence successfully masked the lack of genuine connection with my only living parent. Owen may have joined in on many of our holiday traditions, celebrations, and some of my favorite childhood memories—yet somehow it had never occurred to me before that they were all curated and orchestrated by Grandpa.

I had always assumed that Owen's dedication to keeping me dressed in the latest and most fashionable clothing was a mere overcompensation to my status as a motherless-child. Yet as my eyes have been opened, I understand that his deep psychological need for perfection and presentation was spilling over into every extension of him—which included me, his only child. So what I once thought of as expressions of love—such as manicures and pricey clothing—were, in reality, nothing more than a means to satisfy his own narcissistic tendencies.

As I once shared with Thomas, sometimes the most beautiful of possessions, like my flashy coat from Fireflies Boutique, are merely smokescreens to conceal the *truth*. If you stare at the light emitted from a firefly long enough, you might just miss everything else around you. Though as the months have passed, I have had the opportunity to experience life free from the veil of deception. *A genuine existence.* A life in which a firefly can be appreciated for its beauty, yet not intended to distract from its surroundings. A life where value is found in authenticity.

THE BIOGRAPHER

"You believe Owen killed your mother?" Sadie asks.

"No—I *know* he did," I reply, without an ounce of ambiguity or hesitation.

"Did he… ever admit it?"

"No. *He didn't have to.* The police reopened the case after his arrest. There were several red flags that had been missed at the time of her death."

"Do you know *why* he wanted her dead?" she asks.

"The insurance money—*of course*. He wanted to fund his lifestyle. He wanted to travel all around the world, and that's exactly what he did. Leaving me without a mother. But the money started to dry up eventually—as it tends to do. That's when he began relying on Cece."

Sadie nods. "What did you do once you turned eighteen?" she asks.

"Cora and Leon stayed on as co-managers. And eventually Ben took over for his mother, once she was ready to slow down. I knew that Langley was in good hands once it came time for me to leave for art school. I'd never really experienced schooling outside of my home, on my own. I was ready to live in a dorm, make friends, attend real classes—it was even better than I imagined."

"What about Thomas? Did you keep in touch?" she presses.

"We dated. But once he left for college it was difficult on both of us to maintain a relationship. We decided to just be friends," I reply.

"That must have been difficult. The two of you went through so much together."

"*It was.* He was always there for me after Owen went to prison. No one else could understand the way he did. I had a couple of serious boyfriends during the time I was in art school, but I found it... *challenging*, you know— to open up about my past."

"Did you ever see him again after that?" Sadie asks.

CHAPTER NINETEEN

It's been four years since I left Langley Estates. Cora and Ben have visited me several times since I moved to New York, though their trips never seem to be long enough for me. The three years I spent living with Cora at Langley were more than I could have ever hoped for. Her nurturing disposition and love carried me through as I grappled with the trauma of my father's actions.

Ben quickly became the brother I'd never had, following Owen's arrest. We talk at least a couple of times a week, though I'm surprised to see his name appear on my phone screen when it's already past midnight. He knows I wake up early for work.

"Hey," I answer groggily, once I've located my phone amongst my bedsheets and pillows.

"Greer... I'm sorry to wake you," Ben replies.

I know immediately that something is wrong, so I take a deep, calming breath before responding.

"It's okay. *What happened?*" I ask cautiously.

"Leon has passed away. He was having a lot of pain in his chest this evening, so Mom and I took him to the hospital. We waited for him, thinking he would need a ride home–but instead a doctor came out to speak to us not long after, and broke the news."

I rub my face, hoping to discover that I'm still asleep. Yet as the seconds pass, I realize I'm now more awake and alert than ever.

"*My goodness...* I thought he was doing well since he retired. It's only been... *what?* Six months, maybe," I respond in disbelief. "He turned over all of his estate duties to you, didn't he?"

"Yes, he did. He seemed to be enjoying himself. He'd walk to the house nearly every day to drink coffee and visit with Mom," Ben replies solemnly.

"I spoke to him about a week ago. He told me he'd joined a 'senior social' of some kind. He... sounded great," I add.

"He really *was* doing great. I... don't understand it. But I suppose we can be thankful that he spent the last years of his life at peace. As you know, that wasn't always the case for him. His position as manager was pretty much a dream come true–it gave him so much purpose. And when he decided it was time to retire, well–you know how thankful he was that you gifted him the cottage. He got to live out his days in the place that he loved the most."

Warm tears begin streaming down my face as I think of Leon. He and I had grown close during my time spent living with Cora. The last few years I called regularly to check in on him, and to get updates on the business affairs of Langley. I suddenly feel worse than ever that I never did convince him to let me fly him to New York for a visit.

"I'll be on the first flight home," I assure Ben.

***

Cora, Ben, and Anne-Marie have all been so gracious in helping me plan Leon's funeral services. Despite the sad occasion, it feels comforting to be back in my old bedroom—waking up to the smell of Cora making breakfast in the kitchen. I convinced her to continue living at the house once I moved out four years ago. After she handed over her managerial duties to Ben, I hired her as a live-in house sitter for the estate, essentially. Anne-Marie has also stayed on as Langley's housekeeper.

Ben and Leon worked very well together until about six months ago, when I received a call from Leon letting me know that he was ready to step aside as co-manager. He bragged about Ben and the job that he was doing, assuring me that 'the kid' was ready to fly solo. I'm now left to wonder if Leon knew, on some level, that he didn't have much time left, and wanted to be around to help Ben adjust to the position of sole manager.

The celebration of life service passed by so quickly. It seems like the whole town showed up to pay their respects. As I sit in the back of a black limousine, accompanied by Cora, Ben, and Anne-Marie, I watch the town pass by just outside my window. It has hardly changed at all since I left.

"I spotted Thomas seated at the back of the church. He must have snuck in just before the service began," Cora says, just as we pull up to the gravesite.

"Yes, he drove in early this morning. I'm so glad he made it on time," Anne-Marie replies casually. "Greer, I'm sure he'll be ecstatic to see you."

"Yes, I'd like to see him too. I didn't realize he was making the trip," I say with a slight smile.

Though we've kept up with one another through Facebook, and even exchanged texts every so often, I haven't laid eyes on Thomas since I moved to New York. I know that he graduated from college last year, then started a career in advertising. He and Anne-Marie take turns traveling to visit one another, though I know she would have preferred him to move back to town after graduation.

As we make our way to the burial site, I see a man standing just inside the tent containing reserved seating for family members. He is tall, with blonde hair and gray-blue eyes. He looks so… *grown up*. Photos I've seen posted to Facebook simply haven't captured the essence of Thomas Chambers, and the man he has become.

He's wearing a sport coat, dark green tie, and black slacks. As he stares back at me, the memories of our teenage years spent together come rushing back in full force. I recall exactly how it felt when he kissed me for the first time. *My first kiss.*

"*Greer*," he says, wrapping his arms around me.

"I didn't know you were coming," I say, smiling. "Leon would be so glad you're here."

"I wouldn't have missed it; I just had to finish up some things at work yesterday before the weekend, so I can stay in town a few days with Mom," he says, before greeting the rest of the group.

"Well, you must sit with us. We were, *after all*, Leon's family," I say hopefully.

"Sure," he replies.

Following the burial, we travel back to the estate for lunch that was prepared ahead of time by Cora. It feels kind of surreal spending time with all of them together again. I can't think of Langley, or even Aunt Cece, without also thinking of Cora, Ben, Anne-Marie, Thomas… *and Leon*. They were there during the worst moments of my life–and lifted me up time and time again in the months and years following.

Everyone stays late into the evening talking, eating, and playing board games. Thomas and I have time to catch up while sitting in our 'usual' seats in front of the living room fireplace. It's as though no time has passed. Eventually, Ben joins us–offering up a plate of cookies from the kitchen.

"You did a fine job planning the service for Leon," Ben says before grabbing a cookie for himself.

"It was the least I could do," I say, smiling. "He was a good man."

"Try telling that to fifteen-year-old Greer," Thomas says in jest. "She wouldn't have believed you– and neither would I."

I can't help but to laugh at the thought. "Yeah, you and I were not his biggest fans for a while there," I reply in agreement.

"Not his biggest fans?" Ben interjects. "You two were certain the man was evil in the flesh."

"Yeah, well…" I begin, rolling my eyes at Ben, "…sometimes people surprise you."

"*They sure do*," Thomas agrees, staring at me the way he used to.

"Well, he really did turn out to be a stand-up guy," Ben adds. "I just wish sometimes he'd had a chance to... you know, tell Mrs. Cecilia how he felt about her. We got pretty close after he and Mom became co-managers. He actually opened up to me about it one day."

"Why didn't he?" Thomas inquires, glancing over at me once again.

"I think he was trying to do the right thing. After Carl died, he just wanted to be there for her. He didn't want to be accused of swooping in on Carl's widow with the man's body barely in the ground," Ben replies.

I furrow my brow, silently chastising him for his poor choice of words.

"But Carl passed *three years* before Cece," Thomas interjects. "That wasn't enough time?"

"I'm sure it was," I insist. "But I always got the impression that he was just... terrified he'd ruin what they had together–their friendship."

"Well, I know the fact that he helped bring her killer to justice gave him a lot of peace. I don't think he could have lived with himself if he hadn't," Ben says before passing me a cookie.

"That he did," I reply, staring back at Thomas.

"What about Anne-Marie?" Ben interjects, changing the subject. His question is clearly directed at Thomas. "Does your mother date? She never mentions anything–at least not to me."

"Why *would* she mention it to you, Ben?" I tease.

"I think she dates, but never anything serious," Thomas replies with a shrug. "She seems to be content."

"Well, that's good to hear," Ben responds. "I've always wondered if she has been able to make a romantic connection since... well, since Owen."

"Wait—you knew about that?" I ask, confused. None of us have ever acknowledged the unspoken relationship which seemed to have been formed between my father and Anne-Marie soon after he and I first moved in. At least, we haven't acknowledged it to *one another*. Anne-Marie and I did have a conversation about it a few weeks following my father's arrest.

She admitted that she and my dad did in fact have a relationship which she considered to be a bit more than friendship—and certainly more than a plutonic professional relationship. She referred to it as a flirtation, but nothing more.

Anne-Marie confided in me at the time that she felt quite foolish for having allowed herself to fall for him. She wondered if she might have picked up on anything amiss with Owen had she not been blinded by his charm and apparent interest in her.

I, of course, assured her that she was not to blame for Owen's lies and manipulation. It was a way of life for him, and he fooled a lot of people—*including me*. I admitted that I had been both suspicious and unduly critical of her during that period that she and my father were spending a lot of time together. I recall it being very cathartic for both Anne-Marie and myself to get everything out in the open.

"Well, it seemed pretty obvious at the time that they were… friendlier than you would have preferred, Greer," Ben responds.

"I think *that* was clear as day," Thomas quips.

"Wait, you picked up on that too?" I ask, a bit surprised there's anything about the situation that could shock me anymore.

"Are you asking if I picked up on the budding relationship between my mother and Owen? Or if I was aware how bent out of shape you were about it?" Thomas asks with a grin.

"Both," I reply.

"Well in that case the answer is *'yes'*—to both," he answers.

"And here I was all these years thinking I was the only one perceptive enough to pick up on it," I add. "If you knew, why didn't you confront me about it?"

"You loved your father," Thomas responds warmly. "I knew you were just trying to look out for him."

"Well, of course we all realize now that *we* were the ones who needed protection… from Owen. What a fool I was, huh?" I offer.

"Greer, come on," Thomas continues. His eyes are every bit as kind as they always were. "Owen didn't deserve you—but don't ever blame yourself for loving someone too much."

Ben nods in agreement.

CHAPTER TWENTY

The next morning, I wake up feeling as though I hadn't slept at all. The funeral took a lot out of me, and I'll need to head to the airport in a few short hours to catch my afternoon flight back to New York.

I've spent the last several years building a new life for myself—somewhere I knew my past wouldn't follow me. My first semester of art school, no one knew me as the daughter of a murderer. No one knew that I'd recently inherited millions of dollars.

In the past four years—I've graduated, found a job that I love, and even bought a small studio apartment—which I've had entirely too much fun decorating all on my own. I have a small circle of close friends; I go out on dates; I just... *live*, free from Owen and all the damage he caused.

Yet in the past several days, I've come to realize that I may have been guilty of throwing the proverbial 'baby' out with the bath water. The problem was never Langley. And the problem certainly wasn't the people who have loved and cared for me since I was fifteen. Yet, for some reason—I've been hesitant to return. Scared, even.

In my new life, I almost never think of Owen. My brain tucked him away long ago. Perhaps I've feared that returning to Langley would bring back too many memories of him to ignore.

If this trip has taught me anything, it's that I was wrong about Langley. I was wrong to think that the estate would dredge up every painful memory of my father. It has, on the contrary, reminded me of my Aunt Cece, and how she loved me. It has reminded me of the time spent living with Cora, and how she treated me as though I were her own daughter from the moment she was named as my guardian (if not earlier). It has reminded me of the fun I had with Ben and Leon on the grounds, feeding animals. And of course, it has reminded me of Thomas, and the first time I fell in love.

I decide to wake myself up via a hot shower in my old bathroom. Anne-Marie has maintained every room of the house beautifully. The shower is fully-stocked with everything I could have possibly needed during my stay. My bed was made with freshly-pressed sheets upon my arrival. And I have yet to locate a single speck of dust.

After getting dressed for the day, I stare at my reflection as I brush the tangles from my long, red hair. It seems I look more like my mother, Emma, every day. I can't help but wish she could see me as I am now. I hope she knows that I survived the man who took her life, and that I know the truth. I hope she knows that I won't let her be forgotten.

After quickly applying some mascara and blush, I head barefoot down the massive staircase. The hardwood floor beneath my feet vibrates back at me with every step, just as it always has. As odd as it sounds, I get a sense that the home is happy to have me back. Langley is not just a house. It's a part of history.

There were times when Owen and I first moved in that I doubted if the home was truly on my side. Yet I came to realize very quickly after my father's arrest that Langley itself was always pushing me towards finding the truth. A house this special could not have a man like Owen living in it, dimming its light from the inside out.

Now, Langley is loved and deeply cared for by people who appreciate all that the home is, and what it *has been* to so many people who have passed through the doors.

I stop cold upon entering the kitchen. Thomas is sitting at the table, drinking coffee–just like he has so many times before.

"You're here," I exclaim, unable to mask my surprise.

"So are you," he replies with a grin.

"When did you get here?"

"About an hour ago. It's nice to know that some things never change–you still enjoy sleeping late, I see."

I run my fingers through my still-wet hair before taking a seat across from him.

"Where is everyone?" I ask.

"My mom and Cora left for the grocery store a little while ago, and I believe Ben is on the tractor somewhere," he says coolly.

"I see."

"I just stopped by to see if I could take you to brunch, before you head to the airport," he says.

"Well… I don't see why not. I should have plenty of time," I reply happily.

Thomas stands to his feet, and I feel the familiar sensation of my stomach turning over as he moves closer.

"Well, grab whatever you need," he says grinning.

"What, *right now?*" I ask, once again running my fingers anxiously through my hair.

"No time like the present, Greer. And besides, I'd like to make it a long brunch—what about you?"

I smile in agreement before grabbing my purse from the kitchen counter.

Thomas walks out onto the concrete steps leading to the grass below. He holds the door open as he waits for me to slip on a pair of shoes.

As I descend the stairs, I pause when I realize that Thomas and I are now on eye-level with one another, and I can feel him staring at me—just like he used to.

"What?" I ask, looking over at him playfully.

"It's just strange to be back here," he responds.

"*Where?* The house?"

"No. These steps. *With you,*" he replies, his voice a bit lower than before.

"Why is that?" I ask, staring back at him.

"This is where we first met," he says, gently grabbing my hand.

THE BIOGRAPHER

"So, he came to see you before you left. Did you keep in touch after that?" Sadie asks.

Before I have a chance to respond, the front door opens and we are immediately inundated with the sound of my children storming (loudly) into the house. The girls run over for hugs before my husband has even made it inside with all of their toys and treats from their 'day of fun,' as our oldest, Emma, dubbed it.

Our three-year-old, Ruth, is currently balancing an ICEE in one hand and a new 'stuffy' in the other. Emma quickly introduces herself to Sadie before hitting her with several questions, all in rapid succession. Thankfully, Sadie seems to find it amusing, as most people do.

"I'm sorry, honey. We stayed out as long as we could, but they're both ready to crash," my husband says as he empties his arms of all the girls' various goodies onto the kitchen counter.

"*Thomas*—come meet Sadie, *the biographer,*" I say casually as the girls finally head down the hallway towards their bedrooms.

"It's very nice to meet you, Sadie," Thomas says, shaking her hand. "I'm sorry for the intrusion."

"It's no problem at all. Your girls are the cutest," Sadie replies kindly.

"We'll be in Emma's room until you ladies are finished," he says, turning towards me. "I'll put on *Frozen* for them and I promise you won't hear a thing in here.

Though, fingers crossed they'll fall asleep," he says with a grin.

"Thank you, honey. I don't think we'll be too much longer," I reply before turning back towards Sadie, who is currently occupied with taking notes on her legal pad.

"So…" she says excitedly, "you and Thomas got married."

"*We did.* About a year later. He took a job in New York after we'd been dating for just a few weeks."

"Wow, that soon!" Sadie responds.

"Neither one of us wanted to be separated again," I reply. "Then after we got married and I became pregnant with Emma, we decided to move here to be closer to his mother… and Cora and Ben. His agency allowed him to continue working remotely. And he just makes a trip back to the city every couple of months or so."

"And what about you? I imagine you have your hands full with two young children," she asks, once again taking notes.

"Yes, I take care of them during the day while Thomas works upstairs. But I also sell my artwork at a local gallery."

"May I ask…" Sadie begins, pausing.

"What happened to my inheritance?" I ask, knowing what she's getting at.

"Well, yes. I wouldn't think either of you would *need* to work."

"Langley's doing better than ever. Ben has really come into his own as manager. I think he was born to do the job. We also hired a new groundskeeper to help him out. Cora and Anne-Marie still care for the house."

"Then, why didn't you move your family into Langley?" she asks curiously.

"Thomas and I agreed early on in our marriage that we didn't want to rely on my inheritance. Of course, we're very grateful for it. And it's nice to not have to worry about paying for the girls' college education down the line. But we both really enjoy what we do for a living. We love that we get to spend so much time with our kids while they're young. We've... created a life for ourselves. We didn't want to raise them at the estate because... we want them to be humble. We don't want them to know about the money, at least not yet."

"Well, it seems as though the two of you are doing a fantastic job so far. They're sweet girls," Sadie replies. "But I have to ask–does your commitment to raising them away from a life of... luxury, have anything to do with Owen?"

"Yes, it has everything to do with him," I say, breaking eye contact. "We visit Langley often, but the girls have no idea that we own it. They think it's *Aunt Cora*'s house, since she lives there," I say, smiling. "But they do know it used to be their Aunt Cece's house–we talk about her often. And Grandpa Frank. I just... can't risk any part of Owen coming out in me... or in them."

"How do you mean?" Sadie asks.

"I just think that living in a mansion like Langley, spending my inheritance–the lifestyle is just too risky, for

all of us. Owen's blood is coursing through my veins...
and the girls' as well."

"You're afraid of turning out like your father?"
Sadie asks.

"No, *I'm not*. Owen was a very sick person. Still is,
I'd imagine. And I don't think at twenty-nine years old
I'm going to spontaneously develop traits of antisocial
personality disorder. And as for the girls–so far they are
very kind, very empathetic towards others. But we all
carry some degree of greed in our hearts. You just have to
starve it if you want to keep it from growing bigger. *My
own father killed both my mother and my aunt for money*. He fed
his greed until it destroyed him, and everyone around
him."

Sadie nods, seemingly trying to think of what to
say next.

"Well," she begins slowly, "I really admire the way
that you and Thomas are raising your family. Not a lot of
people in your position would do the same. But–do you
think you will *ever* move back to Langley?"

"We've talked about it, and I think we will one
day. *It's home*. Though probably not until the girls are off
at college. Or if, God forbid, something happens to our
Cora before then, we might consider it. We just want to
get past their most formative years before we let them in
on our secret."

"I get it," Sadie responds. "And I'm impressed."

SADIE JORDAN

I've been a professional biographer for over fifteen years now. It all started in elementary school, when I carried around a notebook and pen to record my daily observations. Some may refer to me as a 'people watcher,' in a non-creepy way.

I love to hear people's stories—where they've come from, where they're going. It's fascinating to me what they choose to disclose, and what they choose to hold back. I think I do a pretty good job of putting people at ease, so that they're comfortable sharing.

I've conducted interview after interview—fine tuning my people skills in the process. Some high-profile figures have sought me out personally. I record their stories, and subsequently turn those life experiences into a coherent, organized piece of literature. It's the only thing I've ever wanted to do.

Some find it a bit vain—the idea that their story is special or noteworthy enough to be recorded. But what I've come to realize is that no one on earth has ever lived a 'normal' life; it doesn't exist. Every life is unique and interesting in its own right.

Though I *will* confess, my ghostwriting services are not typically where I find my *favorite* stories. The most interesting and exceptional stories are usually the ones I must seek out. *The ones I have to pursue. The stories that don't want to be told.*

My publisher encourages me to find such stories. Every once in a while, I'll receive a referral. The interview

I'm conducting today was at the behest of my friend, Keira, who was adamant that her neighbor had a story worth telling.

I will admit, when I first laid eyes on the home this morning (with crayons scattered on the kitchen table and board books on the floor in a heap by the fireplace), I wasn't sure what to expect. I wondered what the young redhead sitting across from me could have to say about her life thus far, hoping Keira hadn't oversold me on her suburban neighbor.

Yet over the past two hours I've been pleasantly surprised–captivated, really–by Greer's life story. You wouldn't know it from her modest, middle-class home, or her Chevy in the driveway, that she has already been through so much in her twenty-nine years. Her story is certainly one that needs to be told, even if it does not necessarily *want* to be told.

I don't know many people who would forego a lavish lifestyle in exchange for a simpler existence. And yet, after getting to know her–it makes sense. She wants to bury the darkness, and leave her childhood in the rearview mirror. She doesn't want to give it the slightest opportunity to overtake her or her family, the way it did with her father. She wants the generational curse to end with her.

Yet, from my perspective–I don't think she needs to worry. She is clearly very friendly, caring, and empathetic towards others. I can quite literally see the pain in her eyes when she discusses the loss of her loved ones.

As Greer walks me to the front door, I thank her for sharing her story with me. I know it couldn't have been easy, dredging up all those painful memories—and yet she did it with such grace and poise.

It is then that I notice a small dining room next to the kitchen, which I hadn't paid much attention to before. As we exchange our goodbyes, my mind is a bit preoccupied with the contents of the room. It seems as though Greer is using it as an art studio of sorts.

There are several canvases in varying sizes lined atop the dining table. A large wooden easel rests in the corner. Black and white sketches hang from a piece of twine which is strung across the window.

Then just as I'm about to head out the front door, one piece of artwork in particular catches my eye. It is resting on the floor in a far corner of the room. It is not on display by any means.

The canvas painting is abstract, and wildly different than all her other pieces. She seems to enjoy creating images of landscapes, wildlife, and architecture—typically including bright, vibrant colors—such as her painting of a quaint chapel that is currently being housed in the kitchen.

Yet this particular work, nearly hidden away in the dining room—is quite the opposite. It is the very antithesis of a 'light and sunny' piece. It is undeniably dark. It practically screams pain and misery. It evokes a sense of destruction, with no chance for redemption.

It's as though Greer has reached into the deepest, darkest parts of herself and splattered her pain all across the canvas. There is no glimmer of light in it. *No hope.*

On the surface, the woman I met today is a suburban mom–wholeheartedly content with her life. She comes across as being very honest and forthcoming. *Very genuine.* And yet, she has faced more pain and betrayal than most do in an entire lifetime. Her formative years were littered with deception. It's a bit of a miracle that she's turned out as well as she has.

Greer waits at the door until I've made it safely inside my vehicle. She smiles and waves goodbye before disappearing into the house, probably relieved that our interview has finally come to an end.

As I pull out of the driveway, I can't help but to think, *once again*, of the painting in the corner. The one so different from all the rest. Greer comes across as being the exact opposite of her father, and she seems determined to keep it that way. As she said, she wants no part of Owen to ever make it out into the world again.

Though it does make me wonder–is the painting which embodies death and destruction itself merely an outlet for Greer to externalize her past experiences and traumas? *Or does it represent a small part of the Greer I met today?*

NOTE FROM THE AUTHOR

Thank you so much for reading **Firefly Lies**! If you enjoyed this story, please consider leaving a rating or review on Amazon or Goodreads. Also, you might want to check out my new (YA) Suspense/Romance novel, **The Alternate**:

The lives of two women collide in this electrifying psychological thriller, all wrapped up within the confines of an off-beat contemporary romance.

Although eighteen-year-old Sam has never met her jerk-of-an-ex-boyfriend's new love interest, Maren—their intertwining storylines take the reader on a fast-paced and unexpected ride, told from the perspectives of both characters.

***Maren** is an impulsive risk-taker with absolutely no desire to settle into a quiet existence. Yet the wheels of fate are set in motion when she meets Chad (Sam's former flame), and finds herself intrigued by his rebellious nature.*

*Despite a difficult childhood, **Sam** is a sensible young woman working to establish a life for herself in a new city. However, her aspirations are threatened when she becomes plagued with frequent headaches and memory loss. Still reeling from her toxic relationship with Chad, she finds comfort in Parrish, the very antithesis of her former beau.*

Though seemingly complete strangers, a consequential connection between the two women will eventually come to light—in more ways than one. But will Maren turn out to be a friend to Sam—or foe?

Printed in Great Britain
by Amazon

58880501R00139